THE HALLOWEEN JOKER

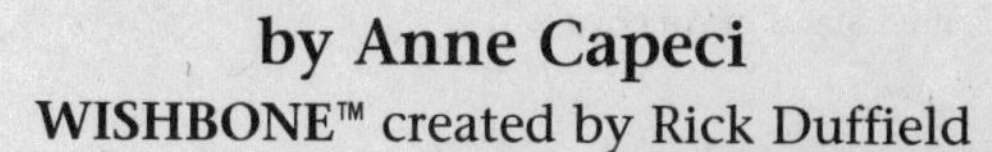

by Anne Capeci

WISHBONE™ created by Rick Duffield

Big Red Chair Books™, *A Division of* ***Lyrick Publishing™***

Big Red Chair Books™, *A Division of* ***Lyrick Publishing™***
300 E. Bethany Drive, Allen, Texas 75002

Edited by Kevin Ryan

Copy edited by Jonathon Brodman

Cover design and interior illustrations by Lyle Miller

Wishbone photograph by Carol Kaelson

Library of Congress Catalog Card Number: 98-85453

ISBN: 1-57064-338-5

First printing: September 1998

10 9 8 7 6 5 4 3 2 1

Printed in the United States of America

For Daniel, the biggest joker of all

FROM THE BIG RED CHAIR . . .

Oh . . . hi! Wishbone here. You caught me right in the middle of some of my favorite things—books. Let me welcome you to THE WISHBONE SUPER MYSTERIES. In each story, I help my human friends solve a puzzling mystery. In ***THE HALLOWEEN JOKER***, Joe, Samantha, David, and I are preparing for a Halloween costume party. But a prankster has other plans—to sabotage the festivities. Can we stop the culprit before the party is ruined?

The story takes place in the fall, during the second season of my WISHBONE television show. In this story, Joe is fourteen, and he and his friends are in the eighth grade. Like me, they are always ready for adventure . . . and a good mystery.

You're in for a real treat, so pull up a chair and a snack and sink your teeth into ***THE HALLOWEEN JOKER!***

Chapter One

"Something tells me this is going to be a Halloween we'll never forget," said Samantha Kepler. She turned to grin at her friend, Joe Talbot. "It's one week from today, and the fun is already starting."

It was a crisp Tuesday afternoon in October. School was out for the day. Sam and Joe walked toward downtown Oakdale. Joe's dog, Wishbone, trailed behind them. The autumn breeze felt cool on Sam's cheeks, and her blond ponytail swayed in the wind. As she glanced down at her sweater, she noticed that its color matched the deep red leaves of a maple tree they were passing.

"Mr. Del Rio sure is going all out," Joe said. He's sponsoring the Halloween party for all the younger kids in town this Friday. Then he's having the scavenger hunt for older kids next week—on Halloween night."

Joe shook his head in amazement. Sam saw that his cheeks were red from the cold. The wind had also tousled his brown hair.

Travis Del Rio owned the town sporting-goods store called Oakdale Sports & Games. Sam had a feeling Mr. Del Rio hoped that by sponsoring special Halloween festivities, his store would get extra publicity. But he also really seemed to want to get to know the people of Oakdale and he certainly liked Halloween.

He had already held a contest to pick the best party theme. And he had asked for volunteers to help set up the party. Sam was impressed with how hard Mr. Del Rio was working to become a part of the Oakdale community. That was one of the reasons she and Joe had volunteered to help out with the party. But Sam had another, even bigger, reason.

"I still can't believe that Mr. Del Rio chose *my* idea to be the theme of the party," she said.

"Congratulations on winning the contest," Joe said. He gave Sam a big smile. "Where did you come up with the idea for Dracula's castle, anyway?"

"Well, I'm reading *Dracula* now. I figured

Dracula's castle would make the perfect setting for a Halloween party," Sam told Joe. "Those old stone towers, on top of a creepy, rocky cliff in the wilds of Transylvania . . ."

"Not to mention the weird stuff that goes on there," Joe added.

Sam had read only a part of Bram Stoker's classic vampire novel, *Dracula.* But already the story had gotten under her skin.

"I think *Dracula* is the scariest book I've ever read," Sam said. "The story begins when a lawyer named Jonathan Harker travels from his home in England to Count Dracula's castle in Transylvania. The count has asked him to go there to take care of some legal business. The whole place seems weird to Jonathan—almost supernatural. But he's young. He's just starting out as a lawyer. So he sees things in a very positive way. He seems to like the count at first."

Joe raised an eyebrow. "Did he realize there was something wrong with Dracula?"

"Not at all," Sam said. "The count tells Jonathan he is the last of a royal family whose roots go back hundreds of years in the eastern European province of Transylvania. At first Jonathan has no reason to suspect anything strange. But soon Jonathan realizes he is locked inside the castle. Then creepy stuff starts to happen late at night. He sees a pack of wolves kill at Dracula's command. Then he has a nightmarish dream about these ghostly women who want to suck his blood."

"Not your ordinary business trip," Joe said.

"Hardly," Sam agreed, laughing. "Jonathan starts to realize Count Dracula isn't just the modern-day relative of an old-time, powerful family. He's a vampire who's been terrorizing the people of Transylvania for centuries. I still don't know what's going to happen to Jonathan, but the situation doesn't look good for him." Sam shivered, then said, "Anyway, it will be great if we can make Friday's party even half as scary as the Dracula tale. It will definitely be a challenge, getting everything ready in just three days. I hope we can do it."

"We will," Joe assured her. "David said he would be at today's planning meeting."

David Barnes was a close friend of Sam and Joe's. He was a whiz with everything mechanical. Sam was sure his scientific know-how would come in handy.

"I heard a bunch of kids talking about the party at lunch today, too," Joe went on. "They said they were coming to the . . ."

All of a sudden his voice trailed off. Joe came to a complete stop, staring at something ahead.

Sam saw that his eyes were focused on an old house that had come into sight. Every kid in Oakdale knew that house. The old Murphy place. It had peeling paint and broken windows. No one had lived there for as long as Sam could remember. Even in the afternoon sun it looked spooky. Rumor had it that the house was haunted. It had been a long time since Sam took that rumor seriously. But Joe looked as if he expected a ghost to leap from one of the broken windows at any moment.

"Joe, are you okay?" Sam asked.

Joe seemed to shake himself into reality. He shoved his hands into the pockets of his basketball team jacket and kept walking. "Yes . . . sure," he said.

"Ooops!" Sam said, checking her watch. "The meeting starts in five minutes. We'd better hurry."

Oakdale Sports & Games was housed in a roomy, two-story brick building that had once been Oakdale's fire house. Travis Del Rio had converted the entire first floor into a sporting-goods shop. From the outside, though, the building still looked like something straight out of Oakdale's early days.

As Sam and Joe jogged up to the store, she glanced through the old fire-engine doorway that served as the entrance. The old fire pole was at the back of the store. The wall behind it was covered with bright flags, banners, and photographs of local and professional sports teams. Sam could see the old firemen's lockers, tucked in beneath the stairs at the far right of the store.

Displays of sports equipment, uniforms, and sportswear were set up around the room. Artificial grass covered much of the floor, except for a strip of exposed concrete at the center of the store. Travis had set up a basketball hoop against the left wall. He'd drawn in the free-throw box on the floor in front of it. The place gave Sam the feeling of being on a football field or a basketball court, rather than in a store.

"Cool," Joe said, as they went into the store. Sam wasn't surprised to see the gleam of interest in his eyes as he looked around. Joe was a good athlete, and a member of his school's basketball team.

Sam saw the group of kids that was standing in the free-throw area. "There's Hank Dutton," she said. "And Amanda Hollings and Sarah Johnson." All three were in the eighth grade with Sam and Joe at Sequoyah Middle School. They were standing with eight other kids near the basketball hoop.

"I don't see David. But he'll probably be here soon," Joe said. "Anyway, it looks as if we have enough volunteers. Even Damont and Curtis are here."

Damont Jones and his friend Curtis were also in the eighth grade. Sam wasn't sure why they had decided to help out with the party. They usually acted as if they were too cool for group activities. But she was glad they had gotten into the spirit.

"Oh, look, Sam. Wishbone is here, too," Joe added.

Sam laughed when she saw Joe's dog, a white Jack Russell terrier with brown and black spots. He was sniffing the artificial grass, his tail wagging as he trotted from one volunteer to another.

Sam and Joe took off their jackets and set them down, along with their backpacks. As the kids gathered around, Travis Del Rio came over from the cash register. He was about as tall as Joe, with dark hair and an athletic build. He smiled at Sam, his brown eyes sparkling with warmth.

"Hello, Sam," Travis greeted her. "You're right on time."

"Hi, Mr. Del Rio," Sam said. "This is my good friend Joe Talbot. He's going to help with the party, too."

"Nice to meet you," Joe said, looking around. "Your store is amazing."

Sam was surprised to see a boy of about nine or ten years of age slide down the fire pole. He ran over to Travis and looked up at him with big brown eyes. "Can I help with the party, too, Uncle Travis?" he asked.

"Sure," Travis said. "Sam, Joe, I'd like you to meet my nephew, Marcus Finch. He and his sister, Melina, live with me in the apartment upstairs from the store."

As Travis spoke, a dark-haired girl who looked maybe a year older than Marcus walked over to them.

"Hi, Marcus. Hi, Melina," Sam said, giving them a smile.

"Well . . ." Travis checked his watch. Then he clapped his hands to get everyone's attention. "We'd better get down to business. Thanks for coming," he said, scanning his eyes at the faces. "There's a lot to do, so let's get started. Sam, why don't you tell everyone your ideas for Dracula's castle? Then we can all brainstorm to figure out how to make it happen."

Sam took a pad out of her backpack. She'd already written down some ideas. Taking a deep breath, she glanced at the list and began. "I thought we could make a big backdrop of Dracula's castle. You know, up on a rocky cliff, with bats fluttering around the turrets and a full moon overhead. . . ."

"I saw a big roll of heavy-duty paper at the *Chronicle* the other day," Hank said. "I'll ask if we can use some of it to paint the castle on it."

Hank had dark brown skin, and brown eyes that were warm and intelligent. Sam knew he helped out at the local newspaper office a few afternoons a week.

"Great," she said. "We should make a graveyard, too, with Dracula's tomb. Maybe we could also make some wolves that are under Dracula's control. . . ."

"Wolves?" Amanda cut in. There was a hesitant look in her eyes. "Do you mind if I suggest a minor change? Something with a bit more . . . drama?"

Amanda had long black hair and a self-confident way about her. Sam liked her, but sometimes Amanda came on too strong. Sam thought the wolves *would* be dramatic. Still, she wanted to be open to suggestions. And Amanda did have a special talent for acting and putting on a good show.

"What's your idea?" Sam asked.

"Picture this," Amanda said. She lowered her voice for effect. "A boiling caldron in the middle of the graveyard . . . Witches dancing around it while they cast their evil spell . . ." Tossing her hair over her shoulder, she hunched forward to show a few sample dance steps.

"Uh . . . Amanda? There aren't any witches in *Dracula,*" Sam pointed out.

Amanda straightened up. "That's too bad, but it's nothing we can't work around," she said, with a wave of her hand. "Especially if we make the castle a *witches'* castle."

"What?" Sam asked, feeling confused. "But that changes the whole party."

"Exactly!" Amanda announced.

ENTER
OAKDALE '88
YOUTH SPORTS
PROGRAM

"Wait a minute. This is all sounding very familiar," Travis said. He turned to Amanda, frowning. "Amanda, you already submitted the idea of a witches' dance when I held the contest. I decided to go with Sam's Dracula theme."

"You're trying to change the party because *your* idea wasn't chosen," Joe said.

Sam saw the way Amanda glared at Joe. Before Amanda could say anything, another volunteer spoke up.

"That's pretty sneaky, Amanda," Sarah Johnson said, shaking her head.

Sarah had shoulder-length sandy hair and was great at track-and-field. Sam liked her. She was glad that Sarah and Joe weren't going to let Amanda get away with changing the party's theme.

"Looks like you're busted, Amanda," said Damont. He leaned against the wall, an amused smile on his face. "You'll have to find another way to make a splash this Halloween."

"But . . ." Amanda started to object. Then she let out her breath and said, "Oh, forget it. If you all can't recognize a superior idea, that's your problem."

With an annoyed shake of her head, she grabbed her book bag and left the store.

Sam stared after Amanda. The planning meeting had started off so well. Sam didn't want Amanda's criticism to ruin everyone else's enthusiasm. After all, Dracula's castle would be a success only if the other volunteers were as excited about the idea as she was.

To her relief, they were. Before long, everyone chimed in with suggestions for the party. Sarah said she could make bats that would swoop down from the ceiling. A boy Sam knew from her social studies class volunteered to rig up glowing yellow eyes for the wolves. Someone else offered to make a tomb and coffin that Dracula could pop out of. Joe said he could help work on creating creepy sound effects—complete with howling by Wishbone. Hank came up with the idea of a Transylvanian miniature golf course.

The only people who *didn't* contribute to the planning session were Damont and Curtis. The two boys kept to the sidelines, looking bored. Sam wondered again why they had bothered to come at all, but she was too busy to pay them much mind.

With everyone working together, the party really began to take shape. In her mind, Sam began to picture how completely creepy Dracula's castle would be.

"What about the fire pole?" Joe asked. "We should definitely use it as part of the backdrop."

Sam nodded. "I was thinking about that," she said. She walked closer to the pole, thinking out loud. "Someone dressed as a vampire could—"

Sam jumped back as a cloud of smoke and sparks appeared at the foot of the fire pole.

"Hey! What . . . ?" Sam cried in surprise.

Suddenly, a dark figure appeared above. Sam caught a glimpse of pale skin, pointed fangs, and a flowing black cape.

Then the figure swooped down the fire pole toward her.

Chapter Two

"Hey! You leave my pal Sam alone!" Wishbone barked at the figure dressed in black that slid down the fire pole. The smoke at the foot of the pole stung his nose and left a bad taste on his tongue. But he wasn't going to let that slow him down.

Wishbone leaped past a group of startled boys and girls. As he jumped closer to the figure in the black cape, his sensitive nose picked up *another* scent. It was the smell of a boy who often visited Joe and Wishbone at their house.

"No need to fear, everyone . . ." Wishbone jumped around the black-caped figure with excitement. "I know who our pointy-fanged friend is. It's . . ."

"David!" Sam cried.

David reached up and took off his rubber mask.

"You nearly scared me to death!" Sam said.

Sure enough, David Barnes stood there, holding a vampire mask. David was one of Joe and Wishbone's neighbors—and a very good friend.

"You should have seen your faces!" David said. He chuckled as Joe, Sam, and the others gathered around him. His chocolate-colored skin was mostly hidden by his cape. His brown eyes sparkled with amusement.

"Good one, David," Joe said. He glanced up at the fire pole. "How did you get up there?"

Wishbone wagged his tail and sniffed at David's

black cape. "Good question. But I've got an even better one: Did you bring me any treats?"

David unfastened the cape from around his neck. "I was just going to leap through the front entrance and scare you. Sliding down the fire pole was Mr. Del Rio's idea," he explained.

Wishbone turned to see Travis standing in the doorway, smiling. "I was putting some empty packing boxes out with the recyclables," he said. "When I saw the costume, I thought there might be some kind of trick in the works. I decided to speak to the person behind the *trick* and find out what he or she had in mind."

"Once I introduced myself and told him my plan," David continued, "Mr. Del Rio let me go upstairs so I could use the fire pole."

"I figured it would be a good way to set the party mood," Travis finished.

"Of course, *snacks* work pretty well, too." Wishbone wagged his tail and smiled up at Travis. "*Nothing* sets the mood better than doggie treats!"

Wishbone had met Travis for the first time that afternoon. Travis had welcomed him into the store like an old friend.

"You set the mood, all right, David," Sam said, shaking her head in amazement. "You really startled us."

"Speak for yourself, Sam," Damont said. He was still leaning against the wall, a sarcastic look on his face. "It takes a lot more than that kind of kid stuff to scare me."

Wishbone glanced up sharply at Damont. He had seen Damont in action plenty of times in the past. Damont wasn't a bad kid. But he *did* have a talent for making trouble, and a habit of acting as if he were better than other kids.

"Well, you scared *me,* David," Sarah said. Ignoring Damont, she turned to David. "You'd better save that costume. I think you can count on being one of the main attractions at the kids' party on Friday."

"Huh?" David said, looking up in surprise. "Actually, I was hoping to do something else for the party."

Wishbone glanced up hopefully at David. "What? Set up a snack table?"

"What's that, David?" Sam asked.

"It's a secret. I can't give any details. . . ." David gave a mysterious smile. "But I *can* promise you that it will be a spine-tingling techno-thrill."

"Techno-thrill? Sounds interesting—but not very appetizing." Wishbone trotted among the other volunteers, his tongue lolling. "We're overlooking something very important here, people. What about the food!"

No one answered. Wishbone trotted over to Sam, but she was busy writing something down on the pad she held. She didn't seem to have heard Wishbone, either.

"Okay, David, I'm putting you down for a mystery surprise," Sam said. "I think we have most of the display ideas worked out. Now . . . what about food?"

"*Now* we're talking!" Wishbone gave a joyful bark. As Sam, Joe, David, and the others started to talk about snacks and drinks, the terrier trotted toward the door. "It looks as if everything is under control here. . . ."

Wishbone gazed outside. The wind rustled through tree leaves that had turned every shade of yellow, orange, red, and purple. Other leaves had dried to a crinkly brown and blew across Oak Street or down the sidewalk. They seemed to call out to Wishbone to chase them. It was a call he simply could not ignore.

"See you in a while, Joe!" Wishbone glanced at his best buddy. Then he trotted through the doorway. "This dog is going for a run!"

The crisp wind felt refreshing on his nose, and it ruffled his smooth fur. Wishbone raced after fallen leaves, chasing first one, then another. Before long, he found himself in Jackson Park. Wide, grassy lawns and countless piles of leaves were spread out before him. There was so much to explore, Wishbone hardly knew where to start.

"Aha!" Wishbone ran after two squirrels that were busy gathering acorns at the foot of an old oak tree. He rolled through leaves and sniffed out burrows, making his way across the park.

He had already been enjoying himself for some time, when his nose suddenly picked up some new smells. "Soggy reeds . . . mud . . . pond water . . ." He kicked up his paws and ran happily ahead. "I'm near the duck pond!"

By that time the sun had sunk behind the trees. Much of the park was hidden in shadows. But the pond was one of Wishbone's favorite places to visit.

"There it is!" He saw the dark silhouettes of dried reeds and some cattails. Fading light sparkled off the still water. Wishbone could hear the croaking of frogs and the rustling of some creature in the reeds.

"Hellllooo! Anyone in there?" Trotting over to the water's edge, Wishbone sniffed at the rotting reeds and batted at some cattails that bobbed above the water. Cattails were some of his favorite plants—though, in his opinion, they deserved a much better name.

Wishbone stopped in the middle of his game and cocked his head to one side. "What's that noise?"

It was a low rumble—not a sound he had ever heard before in Jackson Park. But he *had* heard it on the streets of Oakdale. "That's a truck engine revving up!"

Wishbone knew motorized vehicles weren't allowed in Jackson Park. What was a truck doing *there?*

He trotted quickly toward the noise. Much of the far side of the pond was hidden by trees and some thick bushes. Wishbone didn't see anything at first. But he could hear someone grunting, and—

"Barking!" Wishbone picked up his pace. "Great! A dog . . ."

He had gone only a few more steps when he heard *another* sound not usually heard in Jackson Park. It was the hollow clanging of containers that were banging against one another.

He heard a loud splash, followed by the sounds of a door slamming and the truck engine revving up again. It all made Wishbone *very* curious about what was going on.

Wishbone raced around the bushes. By then

the sounds of the truck engine were fading into the distance. Wishbone saw tire tracks in the sour-smelling mud near the pond. The tracks led away from the water's edge, to a path Wishbone knew well. It wound through Jackson Park and back to the street. Wishbone strained to see some sign of the truck's lights.

All he saw was darkness. The truck—and the dog—was gone.

Wishbone let out a sigh and trotted back to the pond. "What was *that* all about?" he wondered. "Doesn't that person know it's a bad idea to drive back here? Why would anyone want to . . ."

Wishbone paused as his nose picked up a sharp, chemical scent.

"Hmm . . . I've never smelled *that* here before."

He took a few steps closer to the pond. Then

his keen eyes focused on an isolated pool of water near the bushes.

There, half-submerged in the shallow water, lay six plastic containers. Wishbone's fur bristled when he laid his eyes on the slick of milky liquid that was spreading from one of the cans. A slimy gel oozed from another can. Globs of it had stuck to some nearby cattails. The smell coming from it all had a sharp bite that made Wishbone back away.

Whoever was in that truck did this, the terrier realized. *Someone is dumping nasty, bad-smelling stuff into the duck pond!*

Chapter Three

Joe sat back on the artificial grass at Oakdale Sports & Games and tried to listen. Hank was talking about making fake gravestones for the castle's graveyard. Joe heard something about papier-mâché and wire and paint, but his mind kept wandering.

He wasn't thinking about anything special—just thoughts about Halloween. Somehow, seeing the old Murphy place had set his imagination to work. He wasn't sure why.

Get a grip, he told himself. *You're here to help, not daydream.* Shaking himself, he tried once again to focus on what Hank was saying.

"If a few people can help out," Hank told the group, "we can make some gravestones at my house tonight and . . ."

"Gee, Hank," Damont said, rolling his eyes. "That sounds really exciting."

"Yeah. Very cool," Curtis added, in a fake-serious tone. Then he looked at Damont and they both said, *"Not!"*

They gave each other a high-five, as if they thought they had just made the funniest joke in the world. The two boys had been snickering to themselves during the whole planning meeting.

Turning to Damont and Curtis, Joe said, "Guys, no one is forcing you to be here. Why do you keep making fun of the Halloween party?"

Damont shrugged. "Why not?"

"If you're not the center of attention, you're not interested. Is that it?" Sam said, giving Damont a sideways glance.

Sam had made her remark good-humoredly. But Joe could see that she had struck a raw nerve. Damont glanced around moodily. Then he shoved his hands in his jeans pockets and walked toward the store's front door. "I'm outta here," he said. "See you guys later."

"Much later," Curtis added. Then he followed Damont outside.

As they left, Joe could see the look of relief on Sam's face.

"Well, I guess we're about ready to call it a

day. It's getting late," Sam said. She twisted the end of her blond ponytail in her fingers as she checked what she had written down on her pad. "Before we go, I just want to go over a few things. David, you said you have some dry ice we can use, right?"

"Yes. It'll make a really creepy fog atmosphere in the graveyard. And you already know you can count me in for one scary surprise," David added. "Actually, I'd better get going so I can start working on it. 'Bye, everyone."

With a wave, he, too, headed for the door.

As Sam went down her list, Joe made a note of all the things he had volunteered to help with. Just as he was putting the list in his backpack, he felt something nudge his leg.

Joe smiled when he saw Wishbone standing there. "Hi, boy. Where have you been?"

Wishbone barked and jumped around Joe's feet. It was almost as if Wishbone were trying to tell him something.

"Calm down, boy," Joe said. As he bent to scratch Wishbone behind his ears, Joe noticed that his pal's fur was damp. His paws were covered with mud and—

"Ugh! What's that smell?" Joe wondered aloud.

Wishbone's fur gave off a chemical scent. Using some tissues he found near the cash register, Joe wiped Wishbone off.

When he looked up again, Sam said, "I guess that's about it." She was just about to put her pad in her backpack, when the phone next to the cash register rang.

"Could somebody answer that?" Travis called out. He was standing on a ladder, stocking the top shelf of a display of football gear.

"I'll get it," Sam offered, smiling. She went over to the register and picked up the receiver. "Hello. Oakdale Sports and Games."

As Sam listened, the smile faded from her face. "What . . . ? What are you talking about?" she said into the receiver.

Something in her voice caught Joe's attention. She actually sounded . . . frightened.

"Sam? Is everything okay?" Joe asked.

Sam didn't seem to have heard him. "Who is this . . . ?" she said into the receiver. Her frown deepened. She listened a moment longer. Then she hung up.

"What's the matter?" Joe asked. "Who was it?"

"I don't know," Sam said, staring at the phone. "It was a crank call—something about how we'd better watch out for Halloween tricks."

"Uh-oh," Hank said. He raised an eyebrow and looked around at the other volunteers. "Looks like someone's getting a head start on the trick part of Halloween."

Joe saw the uneasy looks on the other kids' faces. "Just because someone made a phone call doesn't mean anything will happen," he said. But as he picked up his jacket and backpack, Joe felt his own sense of uneasiness begin to grow.

He would have welcomed having another person to walk home with. But Sam lived in the opposite direction from his house. David lived right next door to Joe, but he had already left. "It looks as if it's just you and me, Wishbone," Joe said. "Come on, boy."

Outside, the streetlamps cast an eerie yellow

glow over Oak Street and threw long shadows across the sidewalks. Jack-o'-lanterns and other Halloween decorations in the store windows had seemed harmless in the daylight. Now that it was dark, ghostly eyes seemed to watch Joe. He walked quickly, looking back over his shoulder every few minutes, feeling a bit spooked.

Even Wishbone seemed to feel uneasy. As the terrier walked along at Joe's side, he acted nervous. He barked up at Joe a few times. Again, Joe had the feeling that Wishbone was trying to tell him something important.

As they turned off Oak Street, Joe scanned the dark groupings of trees that lined the road. "We'll be home soon, boy," he said. "Just a few more blocks and—"

Suddenly, he heard a noise in the branches of a large maple tree just ahead. Joe felt every muscle in his body tighten, but he made himself keep walking.

You're too old to be spooked by Halloween, he told himself. *There's nothing wrong here.*

The next thing Joe heard was the snapping of a tree branch that made him jump. Before he could look to see what had made the noise, a skeleton dropped from the branches of the maple tree. It jolted to a stop right in front of Joe, with a hollow jangling of bones that chilled him from head to toe.

Chapter Four

Wishbone barked at the rattling bones that dangled in front of Joe. He had been startled by the sudden appearance of the skeleton, its arms and legs jerking in the air. But now he jumped up with curiosity to sniff at the bony feet.

"Hey! This thing isn't real. It's made of plastic!" Wishbone barked. He looked up at its sunken eye sockets—then he shook his whole body. *"Yechh!* That's not the friendliest face I've ever seen. . . ."

Suddenly, Wishbone cocked his head to one side. He stared into the dark mass of trees that lined the street. Then he started to bark. "I hear footsteps! Someone's running away, Joe! Let's go!"

Wishbone took off into the trees. It was too dark to see very well, but he could hear the sounds of sneakers up ahead, crunching over fallen leaves and branches. "You're fast. But I've got twice the leg power. I'm not going to let you get away with scaring my . . . Whoa!"

Wishbone felt his front paws catch on some ivy, tripping him. By the time he scrambled back onto all fours, the footsteps ahead had faded away. The person was gone.

Wishbone sniffed the air, but the person's smell was lost among the scents of evergreen and dried leaves. Shaking the bits and pieces of leaves from his fur, Wishbone found his way back to where Joe was waiting. Joe had taken just a few steps away from the road. He stood there, staring into the woods. . . .

"There you are, Wishbone," he said, still gazing into the darkness. "Who was it, boy?"

"A no-good Halloween joker, that's who!" Wishbone trotted over and sniffed Joe's hand. "I didn't see him and couldn't pick up a scent. But my nose is telling me something now. I smell uneasiness. And it's coming from you, Joe."

Wishbone didn't like to see his pal so nervous. Joe took a long look at the skeleton. "It seems that Sam's book isn't the only place where weird stuff is happening," Joe said. He walked over to the skeleton and reached for the rope that was tied around its neck. "We may as well take this guy

home with us, Wishbone. Maybe we can use him in Dracula's castle."

"Dracula, eh?" Wishbone looked up at his buddy. "Now, *there's* a great story. A classic battle of good against evil. Speaking of which . . ."

Wishbone followed as Joe continued toward home with the skeleton draped over his shoulder.

"You know, Joe, something odd happened in the park a while ago. . . ."

Wishbone had already tried to tell Joe about the containers of milky chemicals. That had been when he'd returned to Oakdale Sports & Games after finding the glop in the pond. Joe hadn't gotten the message then, so Wishbone decided to try again.

He pawed at Joe's leg. "You know that goop you wiped off me at Oakdale Sports and Games? Well, someone dumped it into our favorite duck pond!"

"I know you're hungry, boy," said Joe. His voice was distracted. He kept glancing nervously into the woods. "We'll be home soon."

Wishbone glanced up at Joe in frustration. "Don't you get it, Joe? If we don't clean up the pond, we're talking no more doggie leaps in the water . . . no more chasing ducks and geese. . . . This is important stuff I'm telling you!"

The little dog gave an urgent bark and stopped for a moment, but Joe simply kept walking.

With a sigh, Wishbone trotted to catch up to his best friend. "No one ever listens to the dog."

That evening after dinner, Sam stood on a ladder on the front porch of her house. She held up a white cloth ghost that hung from a string. "How does this look, Dad?" she asked.

Her father, Walter Kepler, stood a few feet away on the front lawn, holding a hammer and nail. A box of Halloween decorations lay on the grass beside him. He looked at the ghost for a moment. Then he smiled and said, "Not bad. The way the wind catches it, that ghost almost seems real. Here, let me put in a nail so we have something to tie that string to."

While her dad went to work, Sam went out onto the lawn and looked back at the house. Decorations of ghosts, witches, and bats covered the front windows. Sam liked the way they looked—spooky and fun at the same time.

"We're just about finished, Dad," she said, bending over the box of decorations. "All we have left is this. . . ." She pulled out a folded-up cardboard skeleton and straightened out its arms and legs and head. "Maybe I shouldn't put it up, after what happened to Joe."

Soon after Sam had gotten home from the planning meeting at Oakdale Sports & Games, Joe had phoned. He had told her about the skeleton someone had set up in the tree to scare him. "Somebody sure is getting a jump-start on Halloween," she said to her dad, as she finished telling him what had happened to Joe. "Halloween is a week away, and already the practical jokes are starting."

Sam's father finished hammering a nail into the porch roof. Then he turned to look at Sam, out on the lawn. "You don't have any idea who rigged up the skeleton?"

Sam had been thinking about that. "It could have been Amanda," she said. "She was pretty annoyed that Mr. Del Rio chose my idea for the Halloween party instead of hers. At today's meeting, she tried to convince everyone to change the whole theme of the party. She seemed angry when Joe disagreed with her."

"You think she might have pulled a practical joke to get back at him?" her dad guessed.

"Maybe," Sam said, shrugging. "Amanda loves to be dramatic. Having a skeleton drop out of nowhere like that . . . It would be just her style. And the phone call to the store ahead of time, to make everyone feel extra nervous . . . I can just imagine her planning the whole thing out."

As Sam spoke, she felt a prickly sensation at the back of her neck—as if someone were watching her. She was suddenly aware of a rustling noise coming from the bushes at the edge of the yard. When she turned to look, however, all she saw were the gray-black shadows of night.

It's really nothing, she told herself. *You've just got Dracula on the brain, that's all.*

Sam had been reading *Dracula* before she and her dad had begun to put up the Halloween decorations. In the book, Jonathan had learned that the vampire spent his days sleeping in a wooden box filled with dirt. Although the vampire was asleep when Jonathan saw him, Dracula's eyes held an evil strength that had scared Jonathan greatly. Now, as Sam stared out into the night, she, too, felt a chill.

"Did the caller *sound* like Amanda?" Her dad's voice broke into her thoughts.

Sam shook herself. Turning back to the house, she saw that her father had finished tying the string to the nail in the porch roof. He gave the cloth ghost a tap. Then he got down from the ladder to join Sam on the lawn.

"The caller had a low voice," she told him. "I assumed it was a boy, but the voice was muffled." In her mind, Sam pictured Amanda as she did her witch's dance for the party volunteers. She had made her voice low and gravelly then. "It could have been Amanda."

Sam turned again to stare into the bushes. Despite the fact that she had on a warm jacket, she felt cold. She folded up the cardboard skeleton and dropped it back into the box. Then she picked the box up and headed for the front door.

"I think I'll save the skeleton for next year," she said. "Do you mind if we go inside now, Dad?"

Sam helped her dad bring the box, ladder, and hammer inside. She was glad to be in the lighted warmth of the house again. She was just reaching for her backpack on the kitchen counter when the phone rang. She reached out and answered it before the second ring. "Hello?"

"I guess you know now that I was serious about those Halloween tricks," said a voice over the line.

The low, muffled voice sent a shiver through Sam. It sounded like the same person who had called Oakdale Sports & Games after the meeting!

"Who is this?" Sam asked, tightening her grip around the receiver.

"That's for me to know, and for you to find out . . . if you can," the voice answered, in a tone that was mocking.

The voice was threatening and self-confident.

Sam tried to place it, but she couldn't tell for sure who the voice belonged to. "Amanda, I know this is you," she bluffed. "Okay, you've had some fun. Now please stop it, okay?"

The person just chuckled and said, "You're not as smart as you think you are, Sam. But I'm going to let you in on a secret. . . . The fun is just beginning. Something tells me another one of your party helpers will be in for a surprise tonight. She can run . . . but she can't hide."

"What do you mean?" Sam asked. "Who . . . ?"

The line went dead before Sam could finish her question.

For a moment, all she could do was stare at the phone. The practical joker's words echoed in her mind. *You're not as smart as you think you are. . . .*

What did the caller mean by that? And why was the person calling *her?* Whoever it was obviously didn't think Sam had what it took to stop him.

Or *her,* Sam reminded herself.

"I've got to do something!" she said aloud. If she could just figure out who the joker's next target was . . .

Thinking back, Sam recalled what the joker had said: *She can run . . . but she can't hide.*

Sam turned the words over in her mind. Then she snapped her fingers. Sarah Johnson was the best short-distance runner on the Sequoyah track team. Was it possible that *she* was the joker's next target?

"There's only one way to find out," Sam said aloud. Grabbing the phone book, she looked up Sarah's number, then dialed it.

Sarah's mother answered. When Sam asked to speak to Sarah, Mrs. Johnson said, "I'm sorry, but she's not here now, Sam. If you'd like, I can have her call you when she gets back from her run."

"Run? By herself?" Sam felt as if a lead weight had just landed in the pit of her stomach.

"Yes. This late she usually runs with her dad. But he could not join her tonight," said Mrs. Johnson.

"Do you know what route she took?" Sam asked.

"I sure do," Mrs. Johnson said, laughing. "Sarah has run it so often, I think her sneakers must have made permanent marks along the way."

As Mrs. Johnson told Sam what the route was, Sam jotted it down. "Thanks a lot," she told Sarah's mother. "Maybe I'll try to catch up with her."

Sam hung up. She ran into the living room, where her dad was reading the paper. "Dad, can you drive me somewhere? It's important."

She told him about the practical joker's second

call. He then agreed that they should try to find and warn Sarah. A few minutes later, Sam was sitting in the front seat of the car while her dad drove.

Sam looked at the route she had written down. Then she glanced ahead to check where they were. "Turn here," she told her dad. She pointed to a street that led off to the left. "According to Mrs. Johnson, Sarah always runs straight to the end of this street. Then she turns right. From there it's just half a block to her house."

Sam leaned forward as they drove, her eyes searching the street, sidewalks, and lawns. Lights from the houses they passed sent a warm glow into the night. But Sam kept focusing on the black blankets of shadows that the light didn't reach. She couldn't help but wonder what lay hidden in

that darkness—trees and bushes and storage sheds? Or possibly something frightening . . .

"No sign of her yet," Sam murmured, as her dad turned right onto the street where Sarah lived.

"We'll probably find she's already safely back at home," her dad said.

"I hope so," Sam said. She pointed to a shingled house on the left. "We're back at her house."

A light at the end of the Johnsons' driveway threw a dim glow across the front yard. As Sam's father pulled up in front of the house, Sam glanced toward the front porch.

"That's weird," she said, frowning. "What's all that fog? Why is it *inside* the porch?"

The Johnsons' porch was protected by big mesh screens that wrapped around the front and sides of it. It was a clear evening, yet the entire inside of the porch was hidden by thick, smoky fog. Wisps of it drifted through the screens into the chilly evening air.

"It *is* odd," said her dad, turning to look.

Suddenly, the heavy feeling in Sam's stomach was back. As soon as the car came to a stop, Sam pushed open the door and got out.

That was when she heard it—a deep, haunting laugh that echoed from the thick of the fog. The sound was so evil that it made goose bumps pop up all over Sam's arms.

Then, before the laughter faded away, a terrified scream rang out.

"Oh, no . . ." Sam said breathlessly. "Sarah's in trouble!"

Chapter Five

Sam raced toward the porch as fast as her legs would carry her. "Sarah!" she cried loudly as she ran toward the house.

She grabbed the door handle, but the screen door wouldn't budge. Sam yanked hard, and then the door finally opened on its creaking hinges. As Sam ran onto the porch, she heard the soft thud of another door closing.

"Where are you, Sarah?" Sam asked, peering into the fog.

Now that Sam was in the thick of the fog, it seemed to be clearing. Two wooden rocking chairs and a table became visible. Beyond them stood Sarah in her running outfit. Her face had lost all its usual color. She stood completely still, her arms wrapped around herself.

"S-sam? Is that you?" Sarah asked in a trembling voice.

Sam turned as the front door to the house flew open. Mrs. Johnson rushed out. A moment later, Sam's father appeared. As they all hurried over to Sarah, Sam noticed that a jack-o'-lantern lay smashed on the porch floor.

"Honey, are you all right?" asked Mrs. Johnson. She wrapped an arm around her daughter's shoulders. She frowned down at the smashed pumpkin. "What happened?"

"I-I'm not sure. I went running. When I came back, there was this weird fog," Sarah said. "I was

going to go inside and tell you and Dad about it, Mom. But then I heard this really creepy laugh." She shivered, her eyes glancing nervously around the porch. "S-someone was right here. I guess the person ran away right after I screamed."

Sam saw that the smoky fog continued to fade away. A thick patch of it remained on one far side of the porch. Sam could make out the outline of a second door just beyond the fog. It appeared to lead to the side yard. As Sam walked toward the door, she spotted a solid lump sitting in a bucket of water that seemed to be the source of the fog.

"Dry ice," Sam said. "Someone played a practical joke on you, Sarah. The person put the dry ice here to make that fog. Then whoever it was got away through the side door after scaring you. I'm pretty sure I heard the door close right when I got here. You didn't see who it was?"

Sarah shook her head, then looked curiously at Sam. "What are you doing here, anyway?" she asked.

Sam told her about the phone call she had received at home. She also explained about the skeleton prank that had scared Joe and Wishbone earlier. "I thought if I got here fast enough, I might be able to warn you—or maybe even catch the joker," Sam finished. "Sorry I didn't make it in time."

"I'm sorry, too," Sam's father spoke up. He gazed at the smashed bits of pumpkin that lay on the porch floor. "I wouldn't mind having a word with whoever pulled this stunt. Destroying someone's property is serious."

"I didn't like being scared half to death, either," Sarah added.

Sam saw that Sarah's face was starting to get its rosy color back. For a while there, the girl had looked as pale as one of Dracula's victims.

Whoever the culprit was, he or she liked to strike after dark, just like Count Dracula always did. Sam had read that the vampire could suck people's blood only in the darkness of night. During the day, he lost his special powers.

Sam had been glad to read that Jonathan Harker had climbed out a window and managed to escape the castle during the day, while Dracula slept. Sam had read of Jonathan's fiancée and friends back in England. Would Dracula somehow find his way into *their* lives? Sam had a feeling that he would. Could the vampire be stopped? Sam had her doubts. He seemed unstoppable.

Sam shivered as she looked into the dark shadows outside Sarah's house. So far the joker hadn't been stopped, either.

And Halloween was still a week away.

Wishbone glanced from side to side as he walked down Oak Street the following afternoon. "Yes, it's another beautiful day to be a dog."

It was sunny, cool . . . perfect weather for romping with his dog pals in Jackson Park. But Wishbone had another, more important mission. He was on the lookout for trouble.

"Anyone seen any trouble? Hmm . . . What does trouble look like, anyway?" Wishbone watched carefully as people came in and out of stores, offices, and restaurants. Just a day earlier, he wouldn't have questioned the smiles he saw on their faces.

But that was *before* he had found out that someone had dumped milky-looking chemicals into the duck pond. And it was before someone had rigged up a skeleton to scare Joe. So far, he hadn't seen anyone or anything that looked suspicious. But he wasn't ready to give up his search.

Wishbone's sensitive nose picked up the smells of cheese and pepperoni as he passed by Pepper Pete's Pizza Parlor. He was tempted to stop in. Sam's dad, who owned the pizza parlor, often let Wishbone sample a few bits of cheese or a new topping he was trying out. But pizza would have to wait until later.

Eyes alert, Wishbone trotted past the Dart Animal Clinic and the Oakdale *Chronicle* building. He crossed the street and glanced inside Oakdale Sports & Games. *Nothing unusual there,* he thought.

As Wishbone rounded the far corner of the sporting-goods store, Jack's Service Station came into sight. "Hmm . . ." Wishbone glanced at a boy who rode his bike up to the air hose. "Looks like school is out. That means Joe is—"

Wishbone stopped short next to the gas pump and sniffed the air. "Hey! Sour-smelling mud . . . rotting reeds . . ." The terrier gave an excited bark as it hit him. "Those scents are from the duck pond!"

A white truck was parked at the gas pump. Wishbone saw that the tires were caked with mud. It had dried and was peeling off in spots. But there was no mistaking the familiar sour smell.

"This is the truck that made the tracks I saw at the duck pond!"

Wishbone ran over to the truck, taking in every detail. It looked brand-new. The paint was glossy and had no scratches. There was clear lettering on the cab doors, along with a picture. Wishbone sat back and stared at the image. A bug lay on its back. Its sticklike legs stuck up into the air. Two *X*'s had been drawn in place of eyes.

"Talk about being wiped out . . . You look like you could use some rest and relaxation, pal."

Wishbone trotted around to the back of the truck. There, in the truck bed, lay several plastic containers. They looked exactly like the cans Wishbone had discovered at the pond. When Wishbone sniffed the air, there was a hint of the very same stinging scent that he had smelled at the pond the day before.

"*Yech!* This smells worse than it does at the vet's—"

Wishbone suddenly jumped back as he heard loud barking. It was coming from the front of the white truck. Wishbone had been so busy looking at the outside of the truck that he hadn't noticed what was *inside*.

He trotted around to the passenger's window, which was open just a crack. A black dog sat there, barking nonstop.

"Hi, there! I don't think we've met before. My name is Wishbone." Wishbone glanced curiously up at the dog. "Didn't I hear you last night at the . . . Hey!"

Wishbone yelped as a shoe pushed him away

Jack's
GAS • SERVICE
TUNE-UPS
PEST CO.
Jack's Servic
OAKDALE
PEST CONT

from the truck. He looked up—then shook from ears to tail. The man who wore the shoe was looking down at him with pale, cold blue eyes.

He had brown hair and a moustache. He was dressed normally enough, in khaki pants and a matching shirt. On the pocket of his shirt was a picture of a bug identical to the one on the truck door. The man had a mean and gloomy look on his face. He seemed ready to explode.

The man didn't say anything. He simply climbed into the truck and drove off. Wishbone ran along behind, barking, but the truck was too fast for him. Wishbone lost sight of it after a few blocks.

With a sigh, he slowed to a trot. "So, *that's* what trouble looks like. Well, you got away this time, buster. But sooner or later, I'm going to catch up with you."

Joe kept his hands in his jacket pockets as he, Sam, Hank, and Sarah walked from Hank's house toward David's house late that afternoon.

"I can't believe you and Sarah both had practical jokes played on you last night," Hank said to Joe. "It's kind of creepy."

Joe just shrugged. He didn't want to make a big deal out of what had happened. "I guess so," he said. "But playing tricks is what people do around Halloween, right?"

At least, that was what Joe kept telling himself. But the truth was, his skin crawled whenever he thought about that bony skeleton dropping out of the tree.

"This is different," Sam said, frowning. "It's one person, going after two kids in a row. And the tricks were creepy, not fun."

Joe nodded. He was glad to know that he wasn't the only one who felt uneasy about the practical jokes. But he didn't see what he and his friends could do to stop them.

"I keep wondering who it is," Hank said.

"And who will be the next target?" Sarah added. "After what happened last night, I'm scared. Just walking to David's house to pick up stuff for the party makes me nervous. I'm glad all of you could come with me."

"No problem," Sam told her. "We have to go to Miss Gilmore's house, anyway. David's house is right near hers."

Wanda Gilmore was a neighbor of Joe and David's. She owned the *Chronicle,* the local newspaper, and she was very active in the community.

When she had heard about the Halloween party to be held at Oakdale Sports & Games, she had offered to donate several bags of old clothes as costumes. Joe, Sam, and Hank had been on their way to pick up all of the things when they had run into Sarah.

As they walked, Joe tried to push all thoughts of the joker out of his mind. *Don't let it get to you,* he told himself. Instead, he tried to focus on what they were doing for the party. "Wanda can be kind of an unusual person," he said. "I bet she has great stuff to use as costumes."

"David told me he was going to be working on his surprise for Dracula's castle," Sam added, as they approached his two-story house. "We'll probably find him in the garage."

Joe thought David's garage workroom was an amazing place. It was filled with electrical parts, old wheels and hardware, and bits and pieces of machines he had taken apart. Today, the garage door was open. Joe saw that David was there, as Sam had predicted. He was bent over something on the cement floor.

"Hi, David," Joe called out.

David straightened up. When he saw Joe, Sam, Hank, and Sarah, he frowned. Reaching for a sheet of canvas, he quickly covered the object he had been working on.

"Uh . . . oh . . . hi," he greeted them. "What's up?" He smiled, but Joe noticed that he seemed distracted.

"Is that your surprise for the Halloween party?" Hank asked. He eyed the mound that was hidden by the canvas. "How about giving us a sneak preview?"

David shook his head. "I told you yesterday—it's a surprise," he said. "What are all of you doing here?"

"I just talked to you half an hour ago, remember?" Sarah said, giving David a strange look. "I'm here to pick up the things you're donating for the party."

"Oh . . . right." David shifted his weight from one foot to the other. He kept glancing at the canvas. Joe knew that when David was working on a project, he sometimes had a hard time focusing on other things. David murmured, "It's all around here somewhere. . . ."

As David began to look around the garage, Joe caught sight of Wishbone standing outside. "Here, boy!" he called out.

Wishbone began to wag his tail. He trotted up David's driveway. The warm gleam in the terrier's eyes seemed to say "I sure am glad to see you, buddy!"

"Wishbone, be careful." David frowned slightly as Wishbone stepped on a pile of old washers that rolled across the floor.

The terrier's paws scrambled, scratching at the cement. Joe saw that there was a tape recorder on the floor right in Wishbone's path. "Wishbone, don't—"

Joe reached out a hand to Wishbone, but he was too late. Wishbone's front left paw stepped right on the recorder. One of the buttons got pressed from his weight. A moment later, an eerie laugh echoed from the recorder's speaker. The sound was so creepy that it sent a shiver through Joe.

"Wow! David, that's spine-tingling," Joe said. "Is that part of your . . ."

Joe let his voice trail off when he saw Sarah and Sam. Both girls were staring at the tape recorder with wide, scared eyes.

"That's it!" Sarah said, in a stunned whisper.

"*What's* it?" Hank asked.

Sam seemed to shake herself. She and Sarah both turned to David with a look Joe couldn't quite figure out.

"That tape recording," Sam said. "It's the exact same laugh that the Halloween joker used to scare Sarah last night."

Chapter Six

Sam stared at the tape recorder, then at David. A troubling question had come into her mind. It was a question she simply couldn't answer on her own. Finally, she turned to David and asked, "What are *you* doing with that recording?"

"Oh, my gosh . . . *You're* the joker!" Sarah said with a gasp.

Sam's reaction was automatic. She shook her head and said, "No way."

"Not a chance," Joe said at the same time.

Sam wasn't surprised that Joe would stick up for David, too. After all, she and Joe were David's best friends. They both knew he wasn't the kind of person who would go around purposely scaring other kids.

"Let me get this right," Hank said. There was

a confused look on his face as he gazed at David. "*You* have the tape recording that scared Sarah?"

"Listen, I know what you're thinking," David said, looking from face to face. "But I didn't do it."

Sam saw the doubting look in Sarah's eyes. "There can't be *two* recordings of the exact same laugh," Sarah said. "If you're *not* the joker, how did you get the tape recording?"

It was a good question, Sam realized. She didn't think for a moment that David was the joker. But . . . "If we're going to find out who *did* pull those practical jokes, we need to find out all we can about the recording," Sam said, turning to David.

"I made it," David said with a shrug. "It's going to be part of my surprise for the party. I recorded it yesterday, after I got back from the planning session at Oakdale Sports and Games."

"How did you get it to sound so . . . creepy?" Hank asked.

"I used an amplifier," David explained. "Plus, I recorded the laugh inside my closet. That made the sound echo even more."

Sam saw that Joe was crouched down next to Wishbone. He frowned and asked, "I don't get it. How could the recording have gotten from here to Sarah's house?"

"Well . . . something weird happened," David said. He picked up the recorder. In his eyes was a look of confusion that raised Sam's curiosity.

"What?" she asked.

"After I made the recording, I left it out here while I went inside to get something to eat," David explained. "Someone must have come in to the garage, because I heard the laugh. When I came out here to check, no one was around, but the tape recorder was gone."

"Well, it's here now," Hank pointed out.

Sam saw the puzzled expression on Hank's face, and on Sarah's, too.

David just shrugged and said, "I looked all

over the place yesterday. And I checked again this morning. The tape recorder wasn't here. What's really strange is that when I came home from school today—"

"You found it?" Joe guessed.

David nodded. "It was right there on the floor, where Wishbone stepped on it," he said. "I figured Emily took it, then put it back. . . ."

Emily was David's younger sister. Sam knew that she sometimes got into mischief. But Sam had a feeling someone *else* was responsible this time.

"I don't think Emily took that tape recording all the way over to Sarah's house," Sam said.

"But *someone* did," Joe added. "Someone who wanted to scare you, Sarah."

"Someone like *David,*" Sarah finished. She crossed her arms over her chest. "If someone else took it, I doubt that whoever did it would bother to put it back."

"I'm not saying it makes sense," David said defensively. "But that's what happened." He didn't say anything more about the practical jokes. Instead, he walked toward some shelves at the back of the garage. "I'll get the stuff you guys need for the party."

"That's another thing," Sarah said. "Whoever

scared me used *dry ice* to make a fog, so I wouldn't be able to see the person. Isn't that one of the things you're donating for Dracula's castle?"

Sam had completely forgotten about David's offer to donate the dry ice. She watched as he opened a small freezer in the garage and pulled out a plastic container. "Here it is," he said. He shook the container, frowning. "Actually, this does feel lighter than I remember. Whoever borrowed the tape recorder must have taken some dry ice, too."

All Sam could do was stare at David. First the tape recording . . . Now the dry ice . . .

"Do you really expect us to believe that person *isn't* you, David?" Sarah asked. "You seemed to think it was pretty funny when you pulled that vampire stunt at Oakdale Sports and Games yesterday. How do we know you didn't have more tricks up your sleeve?"

Sam was surprised that Sarah would suspect David. Then, again, it would take someone very sneaky to take a tape recording from David. Sam didn't know anyone like that. But obviously the joker was someone who knew *her.*

Shaking herself, Sam turned to Sarah and said, "I don't think we should jump to conclusions."

Sarah didn't say anything as she picked up the container of dry ice and a few other items David gave her. But her eyes were filled with accusations. She barely said good-bye before heading back to Oakdale Sports & Games.

Sam, Joe, and Hank said good-bye to David. As they continued toward Wanda's house, with Wishbone trotting alongside them, Sam felt troubled. Whoever had pulled the practical jokes knew her and had called her at home.

Sam bit her lip, staring down at the pavement. *Is it possible,* she thought, *that one of my friends is someone I can't trust?*

Fall leaves crunched beneath Wishbone's paws as he walked toward Wanda's house with Joe, Sam, and Hank. "*I* know David would never do anything sneaky. And you and Sam know it. . . ." Wishbone gazed up at his best buddy. "The question is, how are we going to convince Hank and Sarah?"

If Joe knew the answer to that question, he wasn't saying what it was. He walked ahead, his hands in his jacket pockets.

"We know David, he wouldn't lie," Sam said, turning to Hank. "But the joker sure does have me guessing. . . ."

"The jokes are just getting started," Sam went on. "I keep wondering when and where the joker will strike next. It's kind of like what happens in *Dracula*. . . . The only thing you can be *sure* of about him is that he *will* strike again."

"Talk about evil. . . . That guy takes the prize. But, hey!" Wishbone barked up at his friends. "The Halloween pranks aren't the only mystery around here. It's like I was trying to tell you before, Joe. Someone put some nasty chemicals in the duck pond. Today I saw the man who did it!"

"Calm down, boy," Joe told him. Turning to Sam and Hank, Joe said, "I wonder about something else, too. I mean, why *us?* Why is the joker targeting kids who are planning the Halloween party?"

Wishbone gave another bark, then sighed. "Never mind. I guess all of you have too much on your minds to get the message."

He held back as Joe, Sam, and Hank reached Wanda's porch.

"But *someone* has to keep an eye on the pond. And I'm just the dog for the job," Wishbone said proudly.

With a final bark, Wishbone trotted toward Jackson Park.

"Give my best to Wanda's flower beds," he said. "I'll be back after I rescue the pond from that slimy gunk—and from the bug man who put it there!"

Wishbone trotted next to the colorful leaf piles that dotted the park. He ran past a pair of chipmunks that were burying nuts. He didn't even stop when he picked up the sharp scent left by dogs on his favorite old oak.

"Duck pond, here I come!" Wishbone scooted through a thick hedge of evergreen, then made his way across an open ditch. As he scrambled up the opposite slope, he picked up the familiar smells of reeds and pond lilies, algae and mud.

Wishbone stopped just long enough to grab hold of a small stick in his mouth. Perhaps he could use it to push or prod those cans out of the water.

Up ahead, the pond came into view. The sight of cattails sent Wishbone's tail wagging. But today there was an added treat.

"Ducks!" Wishbone trotted toward the pond with the stick in his mouth. A dozen ducks floated on the surface of the water. Upon seeing Wishbone, they quacked and flapped their wings. Several of them took flight. Another spread its wings enough to skim just above the

water. It headed to the far end of the pond, past the bushes.

"Uh-oh . . ." Wishbone barked out a warning, but the stick in his mouth made it difficult. "Keep away from dere. It'sh dangeroush!"

He was relieved when the duck flew into the air. Wishbone raced along the edge of the pond. As soon as he rounded the bushes, he saw the rims of the plastic cans. The water around them was a cloudy, milky white. One of the ducks had made its way to the edge of the isolated pool. Wishbone saw right away that the bird was in trouble.

Splotches of goopy gel stuck to the duck's webbed feet and wings. The duck squawked and flapped, but it could not seem to rise into the air. Its feathers were so gummed up that it could not fly.

Chapter Seven

Wishbone dropped his stick in the mud. He pictured the cold eyes of the man he'd seen at Jack's Service Station. "Not exactly someone I'd want to curl up next to on the couch . . . Anyone who would do this is bad to the bone!"

Wishbone gazed at the struggling duck as it shook and squawked. Wishbone felt sure it was uncomfortable—and scared. After his experience the day before, Wishbone knew that the chemicals had a stinging bite. The sharp aroma still hung in the air.

Ducks stopped at the pond every autumn on their way south for the winter. But this poor guy didn't stand a chance of finishing the journey—unless . . .

"Wishbone to the rescue!" Moving closer to

the duck, Wishbone began to bark. "You've got to clean that stuff off—and fast! Your only chance is to get back in the water and rub it off!"

The duck seemed startled. It moved away from Wishbone, into the water. Wishbone shooed the creature away from the milky slicks. The duck moved farther into the clean water, flapping its wings.

"That's it! Now, see if you can rub up against some of those reeds. . . ."

As the bird flapped and squawked, Wishbone noticed that some of the sticky substance rubbed off onto the plants. He kept barking until the duck had managed to rub most of the stuff off. Finally, with a hard flapping of wings, the duck took to the air.

"Yes!"

Wishbone jumped up in his best flip. He wagged his tail happily as he watched the duck fly away.

"Now . . ." Wishbone turned his attention back to the plastic containers. Grabbing the stick in his muzzle once more, the Jack Russell terrier began to push the closest one. He knew he could get those cans out of the water, one way or another.

What Wishbone *didn't* know was how he

could prevent the evil bug man from dumping *more* chemicals in the pond.

"Thanks for donating all these clothes for the Halloween party, Miss Gilmore," Joe said a short while later.

"I'm glad to help out, especially for such a good cause," Wanda said.

For the last hour, Joe, Sam, and Hank had sorted through piles of old pants, shirts, and jackets in Wanda's living room. Now, as they stepped out onto her porch, each held a bulging plastic bag. Joe had really enjoyed going through all the stuff. They had even made a vampire by stuffing a black blazer and pants with newspapers. Hank had stuffed an old T-shirt for the head and drawn the fangs with marking pens.

Now, as Joe looked up into the darkening sky, his thoughts drifted in a different direction. Suddenly, he pictured the skeleton from yesterday dangling in front of him. In his mind he could hear the hollow rattling of bones. Then he thought of the old Murphy house, and he shuddered.

Why are the practical jokes having such a strong

effect on me? he wondered. It didn't make any sense. It wasn't as if he were a little kid anymore.

Joe made himself step firmly to the edge of the porch. "Are you two ready to go?" he asked Sam and Hank.

"Definitely," Hank said. "Let's get this stuff over to Oakdale Sports and Games. I have to head for home soon."

"Thanks for everything, Miss Gilmore," Sam said.

Joe blinked as he caught sight of a white blur among the shadows. His muscles tensed. Then he relaxed when he heard Wishbone's familiar bark. "Hi, boy," Joe called softly.

He bent to give Wishbone a welcome pat. But his hands rubbed against something sticky on Wishbone's fur. When Joe looked at his palms, he saw a clear smear of jelly. It smelled bitter and stung his skin.

"Oh, no, this stuff . . . again?" Joe murmured, frowning.

The boy took a closer look. Joe saw that all of Wishbone's fur was damp. His paws were muddy and stained with more of the gel.

"Wishbone, what are you doing on my porch with all that muck on you?" Wanda asked.

Wanda was a very good-natured neighbor. But

Joe knew Wishbone sometimes made her impatient. Joe and Ellen had done their best to keep Wishbone from digging in Wanda's yard. But the active dog seemed unable to stop himself. So Joe made an extra effort to keep Wishbone from bothering her in other ways.

"Off the porch, boy," Joe said.

As Joe went to grab Wishbone's collar, he saw Wishbone was sniffing at ants that were swarming out from a big crack in the porch floor. Joe quickly steered him onto the grass.

"Let's get this stuff off you," he said. Grabbing some fallen leaves, Joe wiped the substance from Wishbone's fur.

"Ugh! More ants," Wanda said. She frowned, watching them make their way across the porch floor. "They've gotten into the kitchen, behind my radiators . . . It's gotten to be such a problem with these critters. I may have to call in an exterminator. There's a new guy some folks at the paper have been saying good things about. I've seen his truck around."

"I think I've seen it, too," Sam said. "Is it white, with a picture of a dead bug on the side?"

All of a sudden, Wishbone jumped back toward the porch, barking. Joe had to grab his collar to hold him back. "Calm down, Wishbone!" he said. "Sorry, Miss Gilmore."

Joe was relieved when Wanda's phone rang.

"Time to get you away from here, boy," Joe said to Wishbone. "'Bye, Miss Gilmore. Thanks again for all the clothes."

As Wanda went inside to answer the phone, Sam and Hank echoed their thanks and said good-bye. They were just stepping onto the grass to join Joe and Wishbone, when the front door opened again. Wanda stuck her head out.

"Sam? Oh—good, you're still here. The call is for you," she said.

"For me?" Sam asked, looking surprised. "Wait up, guys," she said to Joe and Hank. "I'll be right back."

Sam put down her bag of clothes and jogged back onto the porch. As she disappeared inside

Wanda's house, Hank glanced at his watch. "I'd better go ahead," he said. "I'm supposed to be home already. My folks will worry if I don't show up soon."

"I'll tell Sam," Joe said. "See you."

Hank took off down the street with the stuffed vampire under his arm. As Joe watched him go, he suddenly felt alone.

"Here, Wishbone," Joe said. Bending to pick up a stick, he tossed it across Wanda's lawn.

"Joe?"

Joe looked up to see Sam come out of Wanda's house. Her face was pale, and her voice had sounded shaky when she'd spoken his name. "What's the matter?" Joe asked her.

"It's the Halloween joker. He just called me again, this time on Miss Gilmore's phone," she said.

"Uh-oh. How did the joker know you were here?" Joe asked.

Sam shrugged her shoulders. "The joker hinted that one of us is going to be the victim," she said. "I think he's going to strike while we're on the way to Oakdale Sports and Games tonight." Sam had called several party volunteers earlier to meet at Oakdale Sports & Games to work on their projects.

Joe felt himself tense up again. But he didn't want Sam to know how upset the practical jokes were making him. "At least we're together," he said. "So far the joker has struck people only when they're alone."

"That's true." Sam gave him a weak smile. "You know, this whole thing reminds me of *Dracula,*" she said. "After Count Dracula goes to England, he decides to go after a friend of Jonathan Harker's—a young woman. When she's with her friends and family, they manage to keep her safe. But when she's alone . . ."

All of a sudden, Sam's voice trailed off. She looked left, then right.

"Where's Hank?" she asked.

"Oh, no!" Joe said. "He had to leave without us. He's on his way home. Hank is . . . alone."

"Alone?" Wishbone's five senses went on red alert. "Well, he won't stay that way for long. . . . The canine patrol is on its way!"

"We've got to catch up to him, Joe!" Sam said.

Wishbone was way ahead of her. He was already running down the street in the direction Hank had taken. He could hear the heavy thumping of Sam and Joe's sneakers as they followed behind. Wishbone kept his attention focused directly ahead. His watchful eyes scanned the sidewalk and the woods alongside it. At first, he saw only empty pavement and quiet trees and bushes.

Finally, Hank came into sight up ahead. He was passing beneath a street light, the stuffed vampire under his arm.

"So far, so good." Wishbone's nails clicked against the pavement as he picked up speed. "Hang on, Hank! The canine patrol is—"

A small movement in the woods caught Wishbone's attention. He turned his head—and saw something flowing and white about a dozen yards back. The figure was half-hidden by trees, but Wishbone saw a ghostly arm throw something into the air.

"Hank, look out!" Wishbone barked a warning.

Hank stopped and turned to look at Wishbone. In the next instant, something exploded with a *pop!* on the pavement right next to him.

"Hey!" Hank jumped back. Then he quickly covered his nose. *"Yecch!* What's that gross smell?"

Wishbone crinkled up his nose as he caught his first whiff of the odor. He considered himself an expert on smells. But this was a new one—and so foul that he wished he had never come across it. The smell came right from whatever the ghostly figure had thrown.

"A stink bomb!" Hank said, turning to stare into the woods. "Who . . . ?"

Wishbone raced into the woods after the white figure, barking. "Follow me!"

Sam and Joe were catching up fast. "What happened, Hank?" Joe asked anxiously.

"It's the practical joker—he's in the woods!" Hank shouted. "It looks like Wishbone is going after him!"

Voices echoed through the air as Sam, Joe, and Hank dropped their bundles and joined the chase. Wishbone heard the three kids come crashing into the woods behind him. Of course, they didn't have the natural grace and speed of dogs. But Wishbone thought they did a pretty good job of keeping up with him. "This way, everyone!" he cried.

The joker was about ten yards ahead of him. Whoever it was was moving fast and kept changing directions.

"Trying to throw the dog off the trail, eh? Well, it won't work! My nose knows where you are, every step of the way!"

Wishbone kept his eyes focused on the joker's white sheet.

"Yes!" he barked. The sheet had gotten caught

on a branch, slowing down the joker. "I'm gaining on you. . . ."

Wishbone raced forward as the joker stumbled. The white figure moved back and forth among the dried leaves, scrambling to get up again. Wishbone was so close now that he could see arms sticking out from beneath the white sheet.

With a final leap, Wishbone closed his teeth around the fabric. The foul smell of the stink bomb filled his nose. But Wishbone didn't let go.

He shook the sheet—but the ghostly figure gave it a hard yank. Wishbone yelped as he felt the fabric tear loose with a loud *rrrip!*

Wishbone was left with a stinking corner of the sheet in his mouth. *"Bleecch!"* He spat out the scrap of fabric.

When he looked up again into the distance, the ghostly figure was out of sight.

Chapter Eight

Sam's heart pounded as she ran through the woods. *This time, I'm going to catch you,* she thought. *I'm going to find out who you are and put an end to these tricks. . . .*

Under a darkening sky, Sam could barely see the branches that slapped against her arms and legs. The guys had changed directions so many times, she had no idea where they were anymore. Hank and Joe were dark blurs on either side of her. Even the practical joker's white sheet kept fading in and out of sight.

"There!" Sam pointed. She spotted a pale flash ahead and to the right.

Wishbone's barking seemed to get louder. *Way to go, Wishbone!* she thought. *You must be getting closer . . .*

Then, with a final yelp, the terrier fell silent.

"Wishbone?" Joe called out in alarm.

A few moments later, Sam, Joe, and Hank caught up to the terrier. Wishbone was standing in a pile of dried leaves, staring ahead. Sam looked into the thick, shadowy mass of trees. She didn't see any sign of the ghost they had been chasing.

"It looks like Wishbone got close enough to get a piece of the joker's disguise," said Joe. He bent down to pick up a ragged scrap of white fabric that lay on the ground. It gave off the same foul odor that the stink bomb had.

As Sam stared at the scrap of sheet, her hope then faded to disappointment. "But the joker got away . . . again," she said, letting out a sigh. "Come on, guys. Let's go back and get our things."

It took a while before they were able to figure out exactly where they were. As they trudged through the woods, Sam's mind whirled with thoughts. Sam wanted the practical jokes to stop. Even more, she wanted to see the joker with her own eyes, face to face.

Finally, they had almost reached the road. As they came out of the woods, Sam caught sight of the bags of clothes. They had dropped them by the side of the road. Just as she was about to pick one up, her gaze fell on the stuffed vampire.

"Oh, no!" she said breathlessly.

Three words had been written across the dummy's pale face in dripping, blood-red letters: TRICK OR TREAT.

Hank shook his head, staring at the words. "I worked hard on that face. Now it's got fake blood all over it. It's wrecked," he said. He looked angry, and he tugged at his heavy sweater with frustration. "Besides, my clothes smell like rotten eggs."

"You know what scares me about the joker?" Sam said, looking at Hank and Joe. "Whoever it is really seems to *like* scaring us."

"That's true," Joe agreed. "The joker obviously enjoys making a challenge out of the pranks. Otherwise, why bother calling you before he or she strikes? The joker really seems to feed off the attention."

Sam shivered as she replayed the joker's threatening voice in her mind. "What kind of person would *do* this?"

"Beats me," Hank said, shrugging.

Sam shook her head as she thought it over. "I know it's kind of weird, but I keep thinking of Dracula," she said. "And I keep remembering how terrified Jonathan Harker was when he was in Dracula's castle."

"I thought you said Jonathan got away from the castle," Joe said.

"He did. But now I'm at the part of the story where Dracula is going after his friends," Sam explained. "Not only does he drink blood to survive, but he enjoys what he has to do to get it—destroy lives. Then, when some innocent victim dies, he or she becomes a vampire, too."

She looked down as Wishbone pawed her leg. He looked so eager, Sam almost had the impression *he* had something to say about Dracula, too.

"Well, I don't think our joker is quite that bad," Hank said to Sam. "I mean, Dracula is *evil.* The joker is probably just some kid like us."

Yesterday morning, Sam would have agreed with Hank. Sam had always believed that *everyone* was good, at least deep down. Now, though, she was starting to have her doubts.

Sam was still thinking about the Halloween joker when she, Joe, and Wishbone got to Oakdale Sports & Games a short while later. Hank had gone home. As they walked into the store, Sarah Johnson looked up. She and some other party volunteers were painting papier-mâché gravestones in an area under the basketball hoop that had been spread with newspapers.

"What's that smell?" Sarah asked, crinkling up her nose. "Did you guys run into a skunk?"

"Not exactly," Joe said.

Sam and Joe told the others about the latest practical joke. Sam noticed that the kids' faces grew serious as they stared at the fake blood that covered the dummy's face. Hank decided he would not take the costume home. Some kids began to look nervously around. It was as if they expected the joker to pop out from behind the display of basketballs or football shirts.

"That's three attacks in two days," said one girl. She and a few other kids were painting Dracula's castle on some large sheets of heavy paper. The sheets had been taped together so that they completely covered the back wall of the store. "Who could be doing this?"

That was the big, unanswered question, thought Sam. "So far, only one person comes to mind," she said.

"David Barnes," Sarah said firmly.

"No!" Sam shook her head. "I meant—"

"It *has* to be him!" Sarah interrupted. "David knew that the three of you were going to Miss Gilmore's house."

"Yes," said Joe. "But that doesn't mean—"

"All the evidence points directly at him," Sarah said. "David had the tape recording and the dry ice that were used to scare me last night. *And* he saw you right before you went to Miss Gilmore's. He knew exactly where you would be."

As Sam glanced around at the other volunteers, she saw several nods. The other kids actually agreed with Sarah's reasoning.

"*You* knew where we were, too," Sam pointed out. "But no one is accusing you."

"That's because *I'm* not the joker," Sarah said. "*David* is."

Again, Sam saw nods of agreement. It made her nervous to hear the accusations against David. They were so unfair! But the practical jokes seemed to have infected the volunteers and made them extra-suspicious.

"Sarah is so determined to convince everyone that David is guilty," Sam whispered to Joe, taking him aside. "Why?"

Joe shrugged. "She really thinks he is the joker," he said.

"Maybe, but . . ." As Sam watched Sarah, another explanation came to her. "What if *Sarah* is pulling the pranks?" she said, keeping her voice low.

"What?" Joe shot a sideways glance at Sam. "Sarah was a victim herself, remember?"

"Maybe that was just an act," Sam suggested. "Maybe she just wanted to throw us off the track so we wouldn't suspect her. . . ."

"There *is* another person who knew you three were at Miss Gilmore's house this afternoon," said a red-haired boy who Sam didn't know.

"Who's that?" Joe asked.

"Curtis," the boy answered. "He stopped by here at the store, looking for you, Sam. He said he wanted to talk to you about working on Dracula's castle."

Sam exchanged a surprised look with Joe. "Curtis?" she repeated, then looked at the boy. "He and Damont didn't make a move to help us yesterday. Why would Curtis suddenly decide to pitch in and volunteer *now?"*

"I don't know," said the boy, shrugging. "I asked if he wanted to help work on the graveyard, or the painted castle. Curtis said he wanted to talk to you first."

"Well, Curtis never showed up at Miss Gilmore's," Joe said.

The more Sam heard, the more suspicious she became. Raising an eyebrow at Joe, she said, "Maybe he did show up—dressed as a ghost."

While Joe and his friends talked about the Halloween joker, Wishbone trotted to the entrance of Oakdale Sports & Games. He gazed out at Oak Street with alert eyes. Pools of yellow light from the streetlamps fell on the street and storefronts. Beyond were the shifting shadows of evening.

"There's evil lurking in Oakdale—and I'm not just talking about the cat population!"

Wishbone stiffened as he pictured the man he'd seen at Jack's Service Station.

"I'm not going to let that villain make a mess out of my favorite pond anymore." Wishbone started to scratch at the door, looking back at Joe. "Okay, people . . . time to let the dog out!"

"Don't go far, Wishbone," Joe said, as he came over to open the door. "We'll be going home soon for dinner."

"Dinner?" Wishbone hesitated, but only for a moment. "Keep my kibble warm for me, Joe. I'll be back as soon as I can!"

Kicking up his paws, Wishbone ran toward Jackson Park. The paths and woods were dark and empty of people. Wishbone heard creatures skittering among the leaves in the shadows. But he didn't stop to explore. Before long he was climbing the small rise near the pond.

"Uh-oh . . ." Wishbone stopped and cocked his head to one side. There it was again . . . the low rumbling of a motor.

The truck was back!

Wishbone ran faster. Then he paused again when the pond came into sight. Reeds, cattails, and bushes were black silhouettes against the night sky. But Wishbone spotted a dim light at the far end of the pond. It was a flashlight beam, he realized. It came from the same isolated pool where he had found the plastic containers the day before.

The yellow light flickered across the water and trees. As Wishbone crept closer, the beam swept briefly across the face of the man who held the flashlight. In that instant, Wishbone saw the sneaky bug man.

"So . . . it *is* you!" Wishbone crouched low on his front paws and moved closer. He could see the white truck now. The glow from the flashlight lit up the picture of the bug that was painted on the door. The man's dog was prowling around nearby, sniffing anxiously.

The man rested his flashlight on top of the truck's cab. As he reached into the truck bed, Wishbone heard a familiar clanking sound.

As Wishbone came near the truck, the dog crouched down. He leaped toward Wishbone with a vicious bark that took Wishbone by surprise.

"Hey! *I'm* not the enemy here." Wishbone tried to reason with the dog, but the animal kept growling. "Don't tell me the bug man has *you* doing his dirty work, too!"

Wishbone turned as he heard the splash of containers hitting the pond water.

"Take those things out of the pond!" he cried.

Apparently, the man wasn't in a listening mood. Leaving the cans where they lay, he walked quickly back to his truck. He put two fingers to his

lips and gave a shrill whistle. "Get your tail back here, Pepper!" he ordered.

The black dog bared his teeth at Wishbone in a final growl. As the dog ran back to the truck, Wishbone stared sadly after him. "I know it's not your fault. You're just an innocent dog who's been led down the wrong path."

The man was already revving the engine. He barely waited for Pepper to leap up onto the front seat before he slammed the door shut. The next thing Wishbone knew, the truck was pulling around in a U-turn.

Wishbone was still fairly close to the truck. He had to leap to the side as the wheels skidded on the mud. They finally caught, and then the truck sped forward, sending a spray of mud across Wishbone's face.

With a sigh, Wishbone sat back on his haunches. He looked toward the pond. The night was dark, but a full moon reflected off the water. It shed just enough light for Wishbone to see four more plastic containers lying in the shallows.

Chapter Nine

Sam leaned back against the couch in her living room after dinner Wednesday. *Dracula* was open on her lap, and Sam was completely absorbed in the story.

She was quite far into the story now. For the last half-hour, Sam had become more and more worried about Lucy, who was Dracula's latest victim. The vampire had visited Lucy three or four times at her country home on the sea coast of England. Each time he infected her with his evil blood, she became more and more like him. Her skin grew paler, her teeth became more pointed, and her moods were more unpredictable.

At first, Lucy's good friends didn't understand what was happening to her. There were five people close to Lucy: Jonathan, his fiancée, and three young men who were all in love with Lucy. Being very concerned by the young woman's worsening condition, they called in a man named Professor Van Helsing. He was an expert on vampires. With his help, Lucy's friends began to realize that they were up against a terrible force of evil.

Sam was so caught up in the story that she didn't even hear the phone ring. All of a sudden, Joe's voice was coming from the answering machine in the kitchen.

"Hi, Sam. It's me . . ."

Sam's dad was still at Pepper Pete's. Jumping up, Sam ran to answer the call. She picked up the receiver, then hit a button to stop the answering machine. "Hi, Joe," she said. "I'm here. What's up?"

"I just wanted to check in with you," he said. "The practical joker hasn't called you again, I hope."

"Nope. Not since I got that call at Wanda's." Sam brushed her thumb against the pages of her book, which she had carried with her to the kitchen. "I keep wondering who the joker could be," she said. "I know Hank said it was probably just a kid, like us. But I don't know *any* kids who are that mean-spirited. At least, I don't *think* I do."

"It has to be someone who knows us," Joe said.

Sam let out a sigh, thinking about it. "You

want to know the truth? I'm starting to worry that maybe I don't know my friends as well as I thought I did. Maybe the joker is someone I see and talk to every day." Sam frowned down at the drawing of the vampire on the cover of *Dracula*. "That really scares me."

"What do you mean?" Joe's voice sounded confused. "Someone like David?"

"No," she said, shaking her head. "I still can't imagine that. But I guess part of what's bothering me is that I don't feel as if I can trust my instincts about people anymore. I'm starting to think *anyone* could be the joker."

"Wait a minute, Sam," said Joe. "We've got

to look at the *facts*. That's the only way we can figure out who our suspects are."

Sam shook herself. Joe was right, she realized. She needed to put aside the doubts that kept nagging at her. "What about Curtis?" she said. "He knew where we were this afternoon."

"He and Damont made a point of letting us know how bored they were by the whole idea of the Halloween party. Maybe scaring people with these tricks is Curtis's way of making the holiday more interesting," Joe said.

"Or Damont's way," Sam added. "He and Curtis are good friends. If Curtis mentioned that I was at Miss Gilmore's, *Damont* could have made the phone call and thrown the stink bomb."

Sam stared down at the kitchen counter, trying to recall the practical joker's voice. "Whoever it is muffles their voice to disguise it. I guess it could have been either of those two. But I still think Amanda could be the joker, too," she said.

"You mean because none of the party volunteers wanted to change Dracula's castle to her idea for a witches' castle?" Joe asked.

"Yes. She could be pulling the pranks to get back at us," Sam replied. "I tried to tell that to Sarah this afternoon, but she didn't want to hear it. That makes me wonder about *her,* too."

Sam took a deep breath and let it out slowly. "I suspect them all, Joe. But I can't imagine any of them smashing a pumpkin on purpose. Can you?"

"Not really," Joe said. "But we won't know for sure until we catch the joker."

"That might not be so easy," Sam said. "It sure would help if we had some kind of expert on our side."

There was a pause. Then Joe's confused voice came over the line. "Huh?"

"I guess I was thinking of *Dracula,*" Sam said, laughing. She quickly filled him in on what was happening in the book. "Professor Van Helsing taught Lucy and her friends ways to protect themselves against Dracula: using garlic flowers, a crucifix, a wooden stake . . ."

"You think we should walk around with garlic and wooden stakes?" Joe asked.

Sam smiled when she heard the teasing tone of his voice. "The point is," she said, "we have to be careful."

When Joe got to school Thursday morning, the first person he saw was Sam. She was leaning against one of the poles that supported the covered entrance. She stared at every face that passed her, a slight frown creasing her forehead.

"Hi, Sam," Joe greeted her. "Are you waiting for someone?"

"Uh-huh." Sam kept her eyes on the sea of kids moving toward the entrance. "After talking to you, I realized we need to do more to find out who the joker is. I want to talk to Amanda, and to Curtis and Damont. If any of them is involved with the practical jokes, maybe they'll let something slip."

Joe, too, had been thinking a lot about the practical jokes. Actually, he had been trying *not* to think about them. But so far he hadn't been successful. He also thought about all the bad luck he had had on other Halloweens.

But Halloween was still days away. Why was he making himself upset thinking about what *might* happen? He needed to stick to the here-and-now.

"Talking to suspects sounds like a good idea," Joe told Sam. "I'll help."

The more Joe thought about it, the more determined he became to find the joker. If Joe and Sam could put an end to the pranks, maybe all his uncomfortable thoughts about Halloween could finally be put to rest.

"The trouble is, I haven't seen Curtis, Damont, *or* Amanda." Sam let out a sigh and glanced at her watch. "And school starts in less than five min——"

Sam broke off. Joe could see that her eyes were focused on something behind him. Turning around, he saw Amanda riding up on her bike.

"Well, here comes suspect number one," Sam whispered.

Amanda was just parking her bike at the bike rack when they walked over to her.

"Do you have a minute to talk?" Joe asked the girl.

"It's about the practical jokes someone has been pulling," Sam added.

Joe thought he saw Amanda's eyes narrow just a tiny bit. Then she gave a wide smile and said, "Actually, I was hoping to talk to *you,* Sam."

"You were?" Sam asked. "About what?"

"Well, I was thinking about the Halloween party," Amanda said. She took off her safety helmet. Then she flipped her long hair over her shoulder. "I don't think you understand how much fun my witches' dance would be. . . ."

Joe rolled his eyes. *Not* this *again!* he thought.

"A witches' dance just doesn't fit in with the Dracula theme," Sam said.

A stubborn gleam came into Amanda's dark eyes. "If you could see the dance, I'm sure you would change your mind," she insisted.

Sam shook her head. "It's not the right atmosphere for Dracula's castle," she said again. "Sorry, Amanda."

Joe spoke up before Amanda had a chance to say anything more about her dance. "We've been worried about the practical jokes," he said. "You wouldn't happen to know anything about them, would you?"

"What's *that* supposed to mean?" Amanda asked, raising an eyebrow.

"We're just trying to find out if anyone saw anything suspicious," Sam said quickly.

That was a slight exaggeration, Joe knew. What they really wanted to know was whether Amanda had *done* anything suspicious.

"You left Oakdale Sports and Games before the rest of us on Tuesday. Where did you go?" Joe asked.

"None of your business," Amanda answered. She started to frown. But then she let out a low chuckle. "To tell you the truth, I admire the practical joker!"

"Huh?" Sam frowned, gazing at Amanda in surprise.

"Sure. Whoever it is certainly is spicing things up around here," said Amanda.

Joe didn't know what to make of Amanda's comment. If *she* were pulling the pranks, praising the joker could be her way of complimenting *herself*.

Joe turned to Sam, but she appeared not to have heard Amanda. She was looking at Amanda's bike basket.

"Is that a Halloween costume?" Sam asked.

Joe saw a pile of black fabric in the basket. He wasn't sure what it was—until he spotted a pointed witch's hat. "Halloween is next week," Joe said. "It's a little early to be carrying around your costume, Amanda."

"Yes," Sam added, "it's too early for trick-or-treating."

Joe had a feeling he knew what Sam was thinking. If Amanda was the joker, she could be planning to do something much more than just dressing up as a witch and asking for candy.

Staring at Amanda, Joe waited for her to answer Sam's question.

Amanda's only response was a mysterious smile.

Chapter Ten

Wishbone lapped up meaty chunks from his dish Thursday morning. Joe was at school. Ellen had already left for her job at Oakdale's Henderson Memorial Library. As usual, they had left him with a full bowl.

"Excellent kibble." Wishbone gobbled down the last bits. Then he sniffed at the two ginger snaps Joe had left next to his bowl. "And there's even a little bit of dessert. My compliments to the chef!"

Wishbone was just about to bite into the ginger snaps when he heard a familiar barking.

"Pepper?" Wishbone tilted his head to one side and listened carefully. A moment later, he heard it again. "Yup! That's you!"

Leaving the ginger snaps where they were,

Wishbone ran through his doggie door. Then he raced into the backyard and went around to the side yard. There, parked in Wanda's driveway, was the white truck he'd seen at Jack's Service Station and at the duck pond. Its tires were still caked with mud.

"There's the getaway car. But where's the dog?" Wishbone didn't see Pepper at first. But as he trotted closer to the truck, he heard voices coming from Wanda's porch.

"Your prices certainly are reasonable, Mr. Savage," Wanda was saying.

Wishbone stopped short, staring at the man who stood on Wanda's porch with her. "Evil eyes, cold smile . . . It's you, all right!"

"The name's Wylie Savage. . . ." The man gave Wanda a smooth smile. "Please, call me Wylie."

"All right . . . Wylie," Wanda said, smiling back. "I'd like you to go ahead and exterminate. I just want to make sure that no harmful materials will be left out in the open. There are small children in this neighborhood."

"Not to mention cute little dogs!" Wishbone added quickly. He took a few steps closer, and neither Wanda nor the bug man seemed to notice him.

"And I don't want my flower beds harmed," Wanda added.

Wylie gave Wanda another one of his smooth smiles. "Oh—I am *very* safety-conscious," he told her. "And let me promise you that I take every step possible to protect the environment. . . ."

Wishbone gave an angry bark. "Don't believe a word he says, Wanda! He's just saying that to get in good with you. Then . . . wham! The next thing you know, there's more harmful chemicals clogging up the duck pond."

Wishbone circled closer to Wylie. This character was familiar. In the hair-raising story of Count Dracula, Wishbone knew, the vampire could be very polite and charming. It was one of the ways he was able to get friendly with people. They were fooled about what he was really like—until it was too late. All Wishbone's instincts told him that Wylie Savage was like Count Dracula.

The clanking sound of a chain caught Wishbone's attention. He had been distracted from finding Pepper. Now, as he turned his head in the direction of the metal sound, he could pick up the strong scent of dog. Wishbone trotted toward the rear of the truck. Soon he caught sight of black fur.

Pepper was there, chained up to the back of

the truck. But the chain seemed very short to Wishbone. Pepper barely had enough room to move two feet in either direction. When he hit the end of his reach, he strained against the chain, barking.

"So, *that's* what you were complaining about when I heard you before." Wishbone moved closer.

The black dog stiffened when he caught sight of Wishbone. A low growl rumbled from the back of his throat.

"Uh . . . I'm on *your* side, Pepper!" Wishbone quickly backed away from the black dog. He sat back on the dewy grass. He kept well out of Pepper's way. "Okay, your growling is top-quality. And you've got the threatening bark just right. But . . . didn't the bug man ever teach you how to lighten up and just *play?*"

Wishbone found an old rubber ball of his in Wanda's front yard. He grabbed it in his mouth, then went back to the truck. But when he pushed the ball toward Pepper with his muzzle, Pepper didn't touch it. He just crouched forward and growled at Wishbone again.

"Keep quiet, Pepper!" Wylie called out.

Wishbone sighed. He had known Wylie wasn't a good friend to Pepper. Someone had to show

Pepper what a good friend was. "I've never met a dog yet that I couldn't make friends with. It's just a question of finding the right way of getting my message across. I happen to know from experience that a ginger snap is worth a thousand words!"

Wishbone trotted back across the lawn and into his house through his doggie door. He picked up the two ginger snaps from the kitchen floor and then hurried back outside.

The terrier didn't want to alarm Pepper, so he approached cautiously.

"Here, take thish . . ."

Pepper's ears went back. His tail stiffened. He growled again, straining against his chain. But Wishbone noticed that his eyes stayed focused on the two biscuits.

Slow and easy, Wishbone told himself. He went one paw at a time, keeping the doggie bones where Pepper could see them. When he was just out of the dog's reach, Wishbone dropped the biscuits out of his mouth, and they landed right on the edge of the truck's flat bed.

Pepper's ears stayed back until Wishbone had backed away. Then, straining against his chain, he caught one of the ginger snaps in his teeth. As Pepper examined the thing and chewed on it, he kept his watchful eyes on Wishbone. But this time, Wishbone saw more curiosity than suspicion in the look.

"Yes!" Wishbone knew it would be hopeless to try to convince Wylie to clean up the duck pond. But if he could win Pepper over . . .

"When dogs get together, there's nothing we can't do!" Wishbone sniffed happily at the grass, his tail wagging. "There might still be hope for saving the pond. . . ."

Chapter Eleven

Sam tried to fight off her feeling of frustration as she pushed through the entrance to Oakdale Sports & Games Thursday afternoon after school. "I wish we had more time to investigate Damont, Curtis, and Amanda," she said to Joe, who was right behind her. "But we've got a lot of work here."

She looked at Joe over a load of paper, black gauzy fabric, glitter, and paint that she held in her arms. He, too, was holding a bag of supplies and tools.

"I guess checking out suspects will have to wait until after we get Dracula's castle put together," Joe said. "But I know what you mean. We didn't even have a chance to talk to Curtis or Damont yet. And even though we talked to Amanda, I still can't make up my mind about whether she's the joker or not."

Sam sighed as she put down her supplies. Amanda was up to something. Sam could sense it. But would Amanda really go after so many people—just because they had decided not to go along with her ideas? It seemed excessive, even for someone as dramatic as Amanda.

That's the problem, Sam thought. *The pranks seem too extreme for* anyone *I know to be doing them. But the joker could be someone right here. . . .*

Sam didn't realize she was frowning until Travis Del Rio appeared in front of her and said, "Don't feel discouraged, Sam. I know we've still got a lot of work to do. But we'll get Dracula's castle together. You'll see."

"Hi, Mr. Del Rio," Sam said, smiling. "The party is tomorrow night, and we're not close to finished."

Brushing her hair back, Sam looked around the store. For the last few days, she and the other volunteers had been making everything that would be part of Dracula's castle.

Papier-mâché gravestones and bats lay on the floor near the basketball hoop. The stuffed vampire—complete with a new, clean face—was leaning against the pile. Behind it, some heavy cardboard panels for Dracula's tomb were propped up against the wall. More pieces had been painted to look like a cave, which would be built around the basketball hoop. Cardboard wolves lay jumbled together with rolls of paper painted to look like cliffs and woods. There was a pile of bats, skeletons, vampires, and gravestones to be used as obstacles in the Transylvania miniature-golf course. As Sam looked at all the props, her head started to spin.

"How are we *ever* going to organize all this stuff by tomorrow night?" she wondered aloud.

"We'll do it," Travis said with an encouraging smile. He nodded toward the jumble of things that lay beneath the basketball hoop. "You're already off to a good start. As of now, I'm closing the store.

The doors won't reopen to the public until the party. And this"—he tacked a black sheet into place over the entrance—"will make sure no curious eyes get a glimpse of the castle before then."

Hank, Joe, Sarah, and the other volunteers gathered around Sam. She took a drawing from her backpack and held it up. "This shows where everything should go," she said. "We're going to have a central graveyard, where the headstones and howling wolves and some of the games will be. All the other displays and games and stuff will be set up in a circle around it. . . ."

She was glad to have something other than the pranks to concentrate on. Before long, the volunteers had broken up into small groups. Each one went to work on a different area of the castle. Sam was about to start assembling Dracula's tomb. Suddenly, someone spoke up right next to her.

"We're here, Sam. What should we do?"

Sam turned to see Damont and Curtis. They waited, looking at her, as if expecting instructions.

"So, you really *do* want to help out with the party?" Sam asked.

"Sure," Curtis said, shrugging. "Didn't that kid with the red hair tell you I was looking for you yesterday?"

Sam gave both boys a questioning look. She

hadn't had a chance to talk to either of them about what they might have had to do with the practical jokes. She wasn't going to let the chance pass by now.

"Yes, he said you were going to come talk to me at Miss Gilmore's house, Curtis," Sam said. "Why didn't you show up there?"

"There wasn't time. I had to get home," Curtis said. But there was something odd about the *way* he said it. He spoke up too quickly, in Sam's opinion. And he wouldn't look her in the eye when he talked.

"Really?" Sam crossed her arms over her chest. "I don't suppose you made a detour on the way home," she said. "Like maybe to—"

"Sam! Can you help us over here?" Hank called out from across the store.

Looking over, Sam saw that he had propped the stuffed vampire beneath the basketball hoop. Now he and two other kids were taping the huge backdrop of Dracula's castle to the far wall.

"We need you here, too," Sarah called out. She was on a ladder next to the fire pole. Joe leaned down from the opening above, holding a thin rope that had papier-mâché bats hanging from it.

"I'll be right there," Sam called over.

She turned back to Curtis and Damont with a sigh. Talking to them would have to wait for a calmer moment. "There's a lot to do," she told the two boys. "Why don't you two start by helping to set up the headstones and wolves in the central graveyard?"

"No problem," Damont told her. "After that, we'll just lend a hand wherever it looks like someone needs it."

He *sounded* sincere. But Sam still didn't trust him. She watched closely as Damont and Curtis went over to a blond-haired boy who was already working on the graveyard. To her surprise, they went right to work. They pitched in, arranging the cardboard wolves among the gravestones.

"Sam?" Hank called again.

Sam hesitated. Her instincts told her to keep a close watch on Damont and Curtis. But there was simply too much to do. Leaving the two boys in the central graveyard area, she went over to Hank.

"Dracula's castle looks great," she said, glancing up at the painting. The castle was shown atop a sharp, rocky cliff. Bats fluttered around dark, stone turrets. A full moon peeked out from behind scary-looking clouds. "That's exactly the way I pictured it in my mind. Need some help taping it up?"

"We need the ladder," Hank said. "Can't you get Sarah to hurry up?" He frowned toward the fire pole, where Joe and Sarah were still working with the bats.

"They'll probably be done soon," Sam said. But that didn't seem to cheer Hank up.

"Not soon enough for me," Hank muttered. "I just want to get this over with and get out of here"—he glanced around quickly—"*before* anything happens."

One of the girls Hank was working with looked up with a concerned expression. "David isn't here today, is he?"

"He's at home, working on his surprise for the party," Sam said.

"Haven't we already had enough surprises from him?" Hank said under his breath.

Sam felt her heart sink. Working on the Halloween party was supposed to be *fun*. But as Sam looked around, she saw very few smiles. The practical joker had made them all too nervous.

Just like Dracula, Sam thought. The joker wasn't sucking anyone's blood, the way Dracula did. But the person *was* taking all the fun out of the party.

"I'll talk to Joe and Sarah about the ladder," she promised Hank.

As Sam turned toward the fire pole, her gaze fell on the central graveyard. She saw that Curtis wasn't there anymore. But Damont was. He was bent down next to one of the painted cardboard wolves. In his hand were small yellow lights that would be the wolf's eyes.

Sam thought it might be easier to talk to him *without* Curtis egging him on. . . .

"I need to speak to you two. I'll be back in a minute," Sam called to Joe and Sarah. They both nodded.

As she walked over to Damont, she gave him a hard look. Could *he* be the person who was making those phone calls to her? Was *he* the one scaring everyone? She knew Damont could sometimes be a troublemaker. But was he really that . . . bad?

Sam had to find out.

"You know, I was surprised that you decided to help out, Damont," she said once she reached him. "The other day you acted as if the party was a really dumb idea. What made you change your mind?"

"Well, it's a big deal for all of the small kids in town. I just want to help out by doing my part," Damont answered.

Sam gave him a doubtful glance. Damont

wasn't usually known for his generous, giving nature. But she decided to let the comment pass.

"You're not a little nervous?" she asked. "The practical joker has been targeting kids who are working on the party."

"The joker doesn't scare me. I can handle myself. The question is . . ."—Damont flashed Sam a mysterious smile—". . . can *you?"*

With that, he straightened up and walked away.

Sam stood there, staring after him as he went. Damont's last comment had seemed so . . . threatening. It was as if he were challenging her. "That's just like Damont . . . and just like the joker," she said, thinking out loud.

Sam found herself staring at the dark turrets of Dracula's castle. In her book, Dracula kept finding more and more ways to get to Lucy and drink her blood. Despite all the efforts made by Professor Van Helsing and the others to keep the vampire away from Lucy, he managed to slip past their defenses. It looked like there was no way to stop a force that was so evil and so powerful.

Would the joker triumph, too?

Sam was starting to think so.

At that moment, Wishbone trotted down Oak Street toward Oakdale Sports and Games. He stopped to sniff at the trunk of his favorite tree. Then he continued along the sidewalk. "Pepper is starting to trust me. The next step is to get him to help me keep Wylie Savage from dumping more cans in the duck pond."

Wishbone had taken a brief nap after Pepper had left Wanda's driveway. Now, he was ready to help Joe, Sam, and the other volunteers with Dracula's castle. . . .

"Hmm . . . What's this?" Wishbone paused

outside Oakdale Sports & Games. The entrance was closed, and the door had been covered up with a big black sheet. "How can I help if I can't even get in!"

Wishbone began to bark.

"There's been a mistake! Surely you didn't mean to lock out the canine patrol."

A moment later, Sam pulled aside the sheet and let him in. "I thought I heard barking. Come on in, Wishbone."

"Thanks, Sam!" Wishbone gave her a big smile. For the first time Wishbone could remember, his good friend Sam didn't smile back. "What's wrong, Sam? Has the Halloween joker been—"

"Hold the door!" a voice called out from behind Wishbone.

Wishbone turned around. He frowned when he spotted Amanda. "Isn't she also one of your suspects, Sam?"

"Hi, Amanda," Sam said. "I'm surprised to see you here. Did you come to help?"

Amanda walked into the store ahead of Wishbone. "Hmm? . . . Oh—I didn't want to miss any of the action, that's all," she said. She gazed around at all of the party preparations that were going on. "You know what I mean—when the practical joker has his next triumph."

Wishbone could see Sam's expression darken. "What makes you think the joker is a *he?"* she asked. "It could be a *she,* you know."

Amanda completely ignored Sam's questioning look. "He . . . she . . . whatever," Amanda said.

"Besides," Sam went on, "there's no reason to think anything will happen here today."

"Oh, really?" Amanda raised an eyebrow at Sam. "Well, we'll find out soon enough, won't we?"

Wishbone turned to Sam and barked up at her. "I'm on your side, Sam. If there's evil hiding in Dracula's castle, we'll fight it together."

Amanda walked toward the fire pole.

Wishbone started to follow behind her. "Don't worry, Sam. *I'll* keep an eye on this sneaky creature. If she's the Halloween joker, I'll make sure she doesn't have a chance to strike!" He gave a farewell bark to Sam, then trotted off to catch up with Amanda. "I'm on your trail. . . ."

Just ahead, Amanda wound through the central graveyard. She turned her head this way and that, taking in every detail. Then she stopped to look at the castle, which Hank and a few others were taping to the wall.

"Wishbone!"

"I'd recognize that voice anywhere. . . ."

Wishbone's tail began to wag—even before he turned and saw his best buddy. "Hi, Joe!"

Wishbone looked up above him. As he craned his neck, he saw Joe grab hold of the pole and slide down it. He reached into his pants pocket as he came over to Wishbone.

"I thought you might show up here," Joe said. "So I saved a few of these for you."

Wishbone's mouth began to water when he saw the pretzels Joe pulled from his pocket. "Fighting crime and injustice can really make a dog hungry. Thanks, Joe!"

It was only after Wishbone had gobbled up the delicious morsels that he suddenly remembered the promise he had made to keep a keen canine eye on Amanda. He glanced around quickly . . . but he didn't see her anywhere.

"Uh-oh . . ." Wishbone trotted in the direction where he had last seen the girl. "Red alert! I've got to find Amanda!"

Sam frowned as she looked over the area in the back, right corner of the store, beneath the stairs. The isolated spot was the perfect place for Dracula's tomb. She had already set up a partition to separate the tomb from the rest of the castle. The partition was painted to look like the outside of an old-fashioned tomb—with decorative iron-work and carved-marble details. But Sam had a hard time concentrating on putting the rest of the tomb together.

Amanda, Curtis, Damont . . . All her suspects were right there in the store. But there was so much to do, Sam didn't have the time to pay as much attention to them as she wanted to. Besides, when she *had* talked to Amanda and Damont, they had both been very careful not to say much. Sam was beginning to get very frustrated.

With a sigh, Sam grabbed hold of the card-board panels that would make up two sides of Dracula's coffin. As she angled them into place, they stood several inches over her head. She had a hard time handling them, but she managed to make a corner of the panels.

"Where's the tape that I was going to use?" she murmured. "I know that I . . ."

Sam turned her head as she heard soft foot-steps on the other side of the cardboard coffin. All of a sudden, Sam's skin felt prickly.

"Hello?" she called.

The footsteps stopped. But whoever it was didn't say anything.

"W-who is it!" Sam said. She had meant to sound forceful, but somehow the words had come out in a shaky voice.

Sam heard the shuffling of the person's feet. Then came the low, muffled voice she had come to know so well: "Oh, I think you know who it is. . . ."

Sam felt her heart leap into her throat. It was the joker! Right there in the store with her!

Do something! she thought desperately.

The sound of the joker's footsteps jolted Sam into action. She let the bulky panels fall to the floor. As soon as the cardboard wasn't blocking her vision, her eyes flew around the darkened space.

"Gone," she murmured.

Except for the old firemen's lockers, which were set into the wall, the tomb area was empty. But the joker couldn't have gone far. . . .

Three long strides took Sam to the partition that closed off the alcove. As she came around the partition—

"Ooomph!" Sam collided with someone who was coming the other way.

Sam jumped back, then stared in surprise at the other person.

"Amanda?"

Chapter Twelve

"Not there . . . not there . . ."

Wishbone trotted quickly through Oakdale Sports & Games, looking in every direction for Amanda. He had already peeked into a bat cave and sniffed around the fire pole. Now he was crossing the central graveyard.

"Excuse me." Wishbone gave a friendly nod to the cardboard wolves that dotted the graveyard. "Have any of you guys seen Amanda? Hmm . . . You're not talking, huh?"

Up ahead were three large papier-mâché gravestones that stood in a row. Wishbone circled around them and . . .

"Aha! *There* you are!" Wishbone barked when he caught sight of Amanda. She stood face to face with Sam at the edge of the graveyard. Behind them was a screen that had been painted to look like a dark, scary tomb. "Hi, Sam! I guess *you're* keeping an eye on Amanda now, huh?"

Wishbone glanced curiously back and forth between the two girls. Sam frowned darkly at Amanda, her arms crossed over her chest. Amanda stared right back at her.

"You two look serious! Then, again . . ."—Wishbone glanced at the painted tomb next to them—". . . a graveyard isn't the most cheerful place I've ever seen."

"What were you doing, Amanda?" Sam asked.

"Just waiting to see what the Halloween joker has planned for today's fun," Amanda said. "Like I said before."

She stepped away from Sam and started to walk through the central graveyard.

Wishbone followed on her heels. "Hey! Come back. My pal Sam is trying to talk to you!"

Sam frowned as she watched Amanda walk first in one direction, then the other. "I meant, what were you doing *just now?"* Sam called out. "Back in Dracula's tomb."

Amanda stopped moving. She walked back toward Sam and glanced at the painted tomb. "What are you talking about? Did I miss something?" she asked.

"What happened, Sam?" Wishbone hurried back to Sam and made a protective circle around her legs. "I *knew* I shouldn't have eaten those pretzels. . . ."

"Someone was in the tomb," Sam said. "I think it was you, Amanda."

Wishbone glanced up at Sam in alarm. Then he trotted toward the painted tomb. "You mean, the joker was *here?"*

Nose to the ground, Wishbone made his way inside the tomb. He picked up the smells of cardboard, paint, tape, and . . .

"What's that?" the terrier asked. Wishbone lifted his nose in the air, then sneezed. *"Yechh!* We need some air freshener back here, folks." But when he sniffed again, the idea hit him. "That's the same smell that came from the stink bomb!"

Wishbone followed the scent to the very back of Dracula's tomb. There, set into the wall beneath the stairs, were the old firemen's lockers. The horrible odor was strongest next to the bottom locker on the left.

"Hmm . . ." Looking closely, Wishbone saw that the locker door stuck out a fraction of an inch. "Hmm . . . if the latch didn't catch . . ."

The terrier scratched at the corner of the small door with his front paws. After a few tries, he got the door popped open just enough so he could squeeze his muzzle into the crack.

"Once again, the dog performs an act of amazing canine skill and . . . *Yechh!* This is where the smell is coming from, all right!"

Lying in the bottom of the locker was a mound of black fabric.

"Black, huh?"

Wishbone stared curiously at the fabric. The sheet the practical joker had worn when he had thrown the stink bomb was *white,* not black. But as Wishbone grabbed a corner of the black fabric and pulled, he caught sight of a rip that was very familiar.

"*That's* where the sheet tore when the joker ripped it from my teeth!" Wishbone danced excitedly around the fabric. "Even though it's been dyed black, I *know* it's the same sheet the joker wore. I'd recognize that smell anywhere!"

Wishbone grabbed the fabric in his mouth.

"Blech!"

He trotted out of the tomb.

"Sam! Joe! Look!"

"Here's the ladder, Hank," Joe said. He put the ladder down next to the panorama of Dracula's castle. Then Joe looked around the store.

He and Sarah still had half a dozen bats to hang beneath the fire pole. They had run out of string, so Sarah had gone out to buy some more.

"Now I'll have a chance to talk to Curtis," Joe said.

Sam had given Joe a rundown of her conversation with Damont. Apparently, Damont hadn't made any major slips when Sam had quizzed him. But maybe Curtis would.

Ever since Joe had talked about the practical jokes with Sam the night before, he had been feeling better. It felt good to take action. Still, Joe and Sam didn't know for sure who it was. But . . .

Joe frowned as he caught sight of Sam, hurrying across the store toward him. Her face looked tense, and her arms were crossed tightly over her chest. Something was wrong.

"What's the matter?" Joe asked, meeting Sam at the edge of the central graveyard.

"The practical joker just tried to scare me," she told him.

Joe's mouth dropped open. "Right here in the store? With all these people around?"

Sam nodded. "I was working on Dracula's tomb, and behind the panels . . ." She stopped and took a deep breath, then let it out. "All of a sudden the joker said something, just to make sure I knew who it was."

"Talk about having a lot of nerve . . ." Joe never would have imagined that the joker would strike right in the middle of a group of people. He tried to shake away the unsettled feeling that started to spread over him.

"Did you *see* the joker?" Joe asked Sam.

Sam shook her head. "Not while I was inside the tomb," she said. "But the first person I ran into when I got out was Amanda. She—" Suddenly, Sam broke off and looked down. "Wishbone?"

Sure enough, there was Wishbone, standing at their feet. He held a piece of black cloth in his teeth. The ends of it dragged along the floor behind him.

"What do you have there, boy?" Joe bent down and took the cloth from Wishbone. Then he sniffed it. "Rotten eggs," he murmured, screwing up his nose. "Just like . . ."

"The stink bomb," Sam finished.

Joe examined the black cloth. "It looks like some kind of homemade cape," he said, thinking out loud.

Sam crouched down next to him. Joe saw a gleam in her eyes as she fingered a rough rip at one edge of the cape. "Joe, remember how Wishbone tore off a piece from the joker's sheet after he threw the stink bomb last night?"

"You think this is it, just dyed black?" Joe asked.

Wishbone barked up at Joe. He seemed excited about the cape.

"Where did you find this, boy?" Joe asked, holding the cape out to Wishbone. "Can you show us?"

Wishbone was already trotting across the central graveyard. Joe and Sam followed him past a partition that had been painted to look like the outside of Dracula's tomb. Inside the tomb, Joe saw some cardboard panels that looked like Dracula's coffin. Wishbone trotted past them to an open locker that was set into the wall. He pawed at it, looking up at Joe and Sam.

"Is this where you found the cape?" Joe asked. When Wishbone barked again, Joe smiled at him. "Good work, boy!"

Sam stared at the locker with puzzled eyes. "I don't get it. The joker must have put the cape in there while he was back here. But . . . why?" she asked. "And why didn't I get a warning call before the joker struck again?"

Joe wasn't sure what to think. "You said you saw Amanda?" he asked.

Sam glanced at the doorway to the tomb. "She was right out there just after I heard the joker," she said. "Did you see her?"

"No. I was busy hooking up the bats by the fire pole. I didn't notice what she was doing," Joe said.

"What about Damont?" Sam asked.

"Sorry, Sam," Joe said, shaking his head. "I wasn't paying close attention to Damont either. I guess he could have come in here, but I didn't see him."

"Just like Dracula. *He* managed to slip past everyone's watchful eyes, too," Sam murmured.

Joe blinked as his eyes focused on something wedged into the back of the locker. "Sam, look—there's something *else* in there," he said.

Joe reached in and pulled out a folded scrap of paper. He unfolded it, then held it out to Sam. "It's a bunch of numbers," he said.

There were seven of them, scrawled across the sheet. Joe's eyes kept jumping back to the first three.

"You know," he said, "those first three numbers are the same as the first numbers in both of our phone numbers."

"This must be a telephone number!" Sam exclaimed. "But I don't understand why the joker would put it in that locker."

"Well . . ." Joe flicked the paper with his thumb and grinned at Sam. "There's one way to find out. . . ."

The two of them found Travis putting colored sheets over some of the store's lights. Travis was concerned when they told him that the joker had struck yet again. He told Joe and Sam to go ahead and use the store's phone to dial the number they had found.

Sam punched in the numbers. Then she

held the receiver to her ear. "It's ringing," she said, turning to Joe with a smile. "It *is* a phone number."

"But *whose* number?" he wondered aloud.

After about a minute, Sam shrugged and hung up. "No answer," she said. "I guess we're back to square one now. We still don't know who put this number and the cape in that locker—*or* why."

"Cape? Locker?" a girl's voice said behind Joe.

Joe turned to see Sarah standing behind him. She held a small paper bag. She looked back and forth between Joe and Sam with questioning eyes. "Something happened," she guessed.

Joe hesitated. He didn't want to upset everyone. But Sarah was pressing him for an answer. Eventually, she got Joe and Sam to tell her about Sam's close call with the joker in the store.

"You act as if you still don't know who the joker is," Sarah said. "It *has* to be David. I have a feeling it's him."

Joe stared at her in surprise. "How can you be so sure about that? David isn't even here today," he said.

"And, Damont and Amanda and Curtis are," Sam pointed out.

Sarah shrugged and said, "David could have

come and gone without anyone noticing. I just did, when I went out to buy more string."

She held up her paper bag, as if it were proof. But Joe thought her idea was a little farfetched. He hadn't seen a single piece of evidence that connected David to any of the items that had been inside the locker.

So, he asked himself, *why is Sarah still so determined to prove David is the joker?*

"Coming to Pepper Pete's was a great idea, Sam," Hank said Thursday evening. "That pizza looks really good."

"*And* it's on the house." Sam's father stopped in front of the table where Sam, Hank, Joe, and Wishbone sat. As he set down the tray he held, Sam saw big slices of spicy pepperoni resting on a mouthwatering, cheesy pizza. "I know how hard you kids have been working to put together the Halloween party over at Oakdale Sports and Games. You deserve a treat."

"Thanks, Dad," Sam said, smiling up at her father.

"Wishbone appreciates it, too," Joe said. He tore a piece from his slice and dropped it into

...one's mouth. The terrier chewed it up, then got up on his hind legs to beg for more.

"Here you go, boy," Sam said, giving him a bit from her own slice.

As Sam's dad went back to the counter, she looked around Pepper Pete's Pizza Parlor. The rest of the party volunteers were scattered among the tables and booths. They all had their pizzas and were digging in. Seeing them laugh and joke around, Sam was glad she had thought of getting together for a group dinner.

"It's a nice to see some smiles for a change," Sam said to Joe and Hank. "People seemed pretty grim while we were working on the party today."

"Can you blame them?" Hank said. "The Halloween pranks are really getting serious. It feels as if everyone working on the party is a sitting duck."

Sam shuddered at the idea Hank had just expressed. But she understood how he felt.

"Especially after the joker got to you today, Sam," Joe added. "Right there in the store, with people all around. It really makes you wonder how much more daring the joker may get."

Joe had hit on exactly what had been bothering Sam. Every time she looked at someone, she found herself wondering: *Could he be the joker? Could she?*

"Sam?" Her father's voice broke into her thoughts.

Looking over, she saw that he was standing behind the food-preparation counter. He held the telephone receiver in one hand and said, "The phone call is for you."

Sam saw the expression of concern in Joe's and Hank's eyes. She had a feeling they were wondering the same thing she was: *Could it be the joker?*

"I'll be right back," Sam said to her friends.

She walked over to the counter and took the phone.

"Hello?" Sam said.

"Well, well . . . We speak again . . ." The voice that came over the telephone line was low and muffled. It was the joker, all right. Samantha found herself shivering at the cold tone in the person's voice.

"We've all had enough of your practical jokes," Sam said. "If you think you're going to get away with this, you're wrong."

"We'll see about that," the joker told her.

Sam frowned into the phone. "What are you talking about?"

"It's going to be a very *interesting* walk home for one of the party volunteers," the joker said.

"We'll see how cool the monster is . . . after he's had a taste of *my* medicine."

With that, the line went dead.

Sam stared at the phone, trying to make some sense of the joker's words. *We'll see how cool the monster is . . .*

"Monster?" Sam wondered aloud. "Damont?" The name itself sort of sounded like *monster.* Damont certainly liked to act cool. Was that what the joker was referring to when mentioning a monster?

Sam's gaze flew to the booths that lined one wall of the pizza parlor. She was certain Damont had been sitting at the far booth. But now she saw that Curtis was sitting there alone. Both boys' plates were empty, except for their crumpled napkins. *Uh-oh,* she thought. *Don't tell me he already left. . . .*

Sam let out a sigh of relief when Damont pushed through the door that led to the restrooms. He grabbed his jacket from his booth, nodded to Curtis, then left.

"Damont?" Sam wondered aloud again.

He was the last person she would expect to be targeted by the joker. In fact, she had thought it was quite possible that he *was* the joker. Still, she didn't want to take any chances. She had to do what she could to prevent Damont—

or anyone else—from becoming the joker's next victim.

Sam walked back to her table and grabbed her jacket from the back of her chair. "I'll be back as soon as I can, guys," she said to Hank and Joe. "Save me some pizza."

"What's going on?" Joe asked.

Sam was already heading for the door. "I'll explain later," she said over her shoulder.

Sam hurried outside. Then she looked up and down the dark street. Damont was already several yards ahead on Oak Street. He was walking fast, his hands in his jacket pockets.

"Damont!" Sam called out, jogging to catch up.

Damont stopped and turned around. "Sam?" he asked, a surprised look on his face. "Aren't you going to hang out with the rest of the kids?"

Sam opened her mouth to tell him about the phone call. Suddenly, something made her hold back. She wanted to protect Damont. On the other hand, if *he* was the joker, this whole thing could be some kind of trick. "I've got a lot of homework," she said. "If you're going home, do you mind if we walk home together?"

It was the truth, even if that wasn't the reason she had left Pepper Pete's. Her homework *had* been piling up since she'd started work on Dracula's

castle. And she and Damont lived near each other, so it made sense for them to walk together.

Damont gave Sam a sideways glance, then shrugged. "Sure," he said, smiling.

There it was again, thought Sam. The smug smile and sarcastic attitude. Did he know more about the Halloween joker than he was letting on?

"I feel safer walking home with someone," she said. "The Halloween joker doesn't usually go after more than one person at a time."

Sam looked closely at Damont, but he didn't react. As they walked, Sam kept glancing around. The awnings outside closed stores created deep, dark pockets of shadows where someone could very easily hide and wait to attack. Sam looked into the black shadows of the alleys between stores. *So far, so good . . .* she thought.

"By the way, thanks for helping out this afternoon," Sam said to Damont. "We really needed the extra help."

If Damont was the joker, talking about the afternoon might cause him to let something slip about the pranks.

"No problem. I really had fun," he said, giving her another self-confident smile. "Helping out gave me a chance to—"

Damont broke off in mid-sentence and looked to his left. They were just passing Oakdale Sports & Games. The store was closed, and the windows were dark. Sam didn't see anything unusual. But Damont's face was tense and alert.

"What's wrong?" she asked.

"Shh!" He held up a finger, his eyes still focused on the store. "Hear that?"

Sam stood still. "Footsteps!" she whispered. They were coming from around the side of Oakdale Sports & Games. And they were moving fast. "Do you think it might be the joker?"

The look on Damont's face was determined—and a little nervous. "Let's separate," he suggested. "You go right. I'll take the left. If the person tries to run, we'll have him surrounded."

Damont took off, disappearing around the left side of the building. Sam hurried to the right. She raced around the corner, then paused. The glow from the streetlights was blocked by the size of the brick building. At first, all Sam saw was shifting shadows. Then she heard a shuffling noise, followed by more footsteps.

She thought of calling out. After all, what if it *wasn't* the joker? But Sam dismissed the idea right away. Any warning might give the joker a chance to escape. That was a chance she didn't want to risk.

Slowly and silently, Sam moved forward. As her eyes got used to the shadows, she caught sight of a dark silhouette. The person was next to a trash bin. If she could just get a little closer, she might be able to take the joker by surprise.

Taking a deep breath, Sam darted forward. She felt a surge of triumph as her hands closed around an arm.

"Gotcha!" she yelled.

Chapter Thirteen

Sam kept a tight grip on the joker's arm. The joker was smaller than she would have expected. Her fingers reached fully around the upper arm as she turned the person around and—

"Marcus? What are you doing here?" Sam said, surprised.

Sam had met Travis Del Rio's nephew a few times while working on Dracula's castle.

"I was just taking the trash out," Marcus said.

There was fear in his voice.

Then Marcus blinked. "Sam?" he asked. He looked confused and alarmed all at once. As Sam gazed at him, she realized that she had made a mistake. She also understood his question.

"You think *I'm* the joker?" she said. "I was

trying to *catch* the joker, and I got you by mistake. Oh, Marcus . . . I'm sorry!"

Sam gave his shoulder a friendly squeeze as they walked back to the front of the store.

There she was, trying to catch the Halloween joker so no one else would be scared. *But what do I end up doing? Scaring someone myself!*

Great going . . . Sam let out a frustrated sigh, running her fingers through her hair.

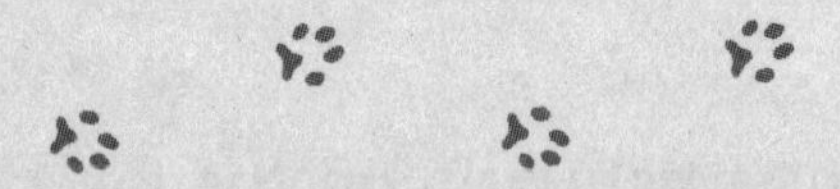

"Hey, Joe! What's the rush?" Wishbone hurried out of Pepper Pete's at his best friend's feet. "Don't you realize there's still *pizza* back there? Joe?"

Joe walked ahead with sure steps, but he had a frown on his face. "Come on, Wishbone," he said. "I know Sam said she would be right back. But I have a funny feeling. . . ."

"I get that way myself. I'm telling you, *pizza* is the best cure—that, or a good belly rub." Wishbone glanced up curiously at his best buddy. Joe's jaw was tight, and the look in his eyes showed worry. "But something tells me that's not what you have in mind."

"If that was the joker calling Sam again . . ." Joe murmured.

"Joker? Why didn't you say so!" Wishbone trotted on ahead, sniffing the cold October night air. "Sam? Are you all right? Hellllooo?" As they went along, Wishbone scanned both sides of the street. "No sign of her so far. . . . Wait!" Wishbone gave a loud bark when he caught sight of Sam. "Over there, Joe!"

Sam was walking from around the side of Oakdale Sports & Games. She had her arm around a young boy. Wishbone started to wag his tail when he recognized Travis's nephew, Marcus. "Hi, guys!" Sam called out.

"Is everything all right?" Joe asked, as he and Wishbone ran over to them. "Sam, was that the joker who called you at Pepper Pete's?"

Sam nodded. "The caller dropped several hints that led me to believe that Damont was going to be the next target. I thought I might be able to catch the person in the act." She frowned and touched Marcus's jacket sleeve. "But I snagged Marcus instead."

"Hmm . . . Something's missing here." Wishbone turned his head from side to side. "Where's Damont?"

"Where *is* Damont?" Joe asked, looking around.

Wishbone sighed. "I just *said* that! No one ever listens to the dog."

"He was just here," Sam said. "We split up when we heard footsteps. I went this way, and he—"

They all turned as Damont came running from around the left side of Oakdale Sports & Games. He kept looking behind him. When Damont saw Sam, Joe, Marcus, and Wishbone, he slowed to a walk and shoved his hands into his jacket pockets. But Wishbone noticed that he didn't stop glancing over his shoulder.

Wishbone sniffed at Damont. "You look as if you've had a run-in with someone, Damont."

"I saw the practical joker!" Damont told the group excitedly. "I tried to nab the person. But whoever it was got away."

"You were chasing the joker?" Sam asked. Wishbone noticed the doubtful look in her eyes. "It seemed to me like someone was chasing *you*."

"Look, someone *was* back there. What difference does it make who chased who?" Damont looked around suspiciously. "Come on. You guys can check it out for yourselves."

Frowning, Damont started to go back the way he had come. Wishbone trotted behind him, along with Sam, Joe, and Marcus. As they entered the alleyway next to the store, Wishbone looked around but didn't spot anything suspicious. He checked out the empty lot and wooden fence at

the rear of the building. There was nothing unusual there, either.

"It *had* to be the joker. The person wore all black, and had some kind of weird hat on," Damont explained. "He came from behind that fence. . . ."

"Say no more. I'm on the case. . . ." Wishbone said.

The terrier sniffed around the edge of the fence. His sensitive nose told him several dogs had left their mark there. About halfway along the fence, Wishbone stopped to smell something that was wedged between two wooden slats.

"Aha! Evidence." Wishbone clamped his teeth around a black object and pulled it free of the fence. "Look at this, everyone."

"Hey! Wishbone has found something," Joe said.

"A hat," Sam said.

Wishbone looked up to see her frowning at the object that drooped from his muzzle.

"A *witch's* hat!" Sam cried.

Wishbone let the black hat fall to the ground. The cone-shaped hat was really ugly, in his opinion. It was a well-known fact that *cats* were the favorite friends of witches. They obviously showed poor judgment—cats, that is.

"This looks familiar," Sam told the guys. Picking

up the witch's hat, she held it out to Joe. "We saw it the other morning at school."

"In Amanda's bike basket," Joe recalled.

"Do you think *she's* the joker?" Damont asked.

Wishbone glanced up at him. For a change, Damont *wasn't* acting cool.

"Are you guys thinking the same thing I am?" Wishbone turned to Sam and Joe. "Maybe Damont isn't the joker, after all."

Half an hour later, Wishbone smiled up at Sam and Joe as they left Pepper Pete's for the second time. Sam was going home with her dad and Ellen was coming by to pick up Joe. "Mission accomplished. Marcus is safely back at home, the joker's pointy witch's hat is safely stored in Sam's backpack, *and* the rest of our pizza is safely stored in our stomachs." Wishbone jumped up in a satisfied flip. "All in a good day's work, I'd say."

"So, do you think the joker is Amanda?" Joe asked, turning to Sam.

"It seems like she is," Sam said. "But we still don't know for sure. That looked like the hat from her costume. But other people could have one just like it."

Sam frowned and kicked at some pebbles on the sidewalk with the toe of her sneaker. "The Halloween party is tomorrow night and we *still* haven't caught the joker."

"Well, it's too late to do anything more tonight," Joe said.

Wishbone said, "Joe, I'll be home as soon as I check out the duck pond."

Wishbone turned to go, but he didn't get very far. "Stay, Wishbone!" Joe called out.

"But, Joe!" Wishbone turned around and barked at his buddy. "The bug man dumped nasty chemicals in the pond *twice.* What if he comes back again tonight?"

The eager dog took a few steps away, but Joe caught him by the collar.

"Wishbone has been running off a lot lately," Joe told Sam. "And every time he comes back, he's got this awful, sticky, smelly stuff on him. I'm afraid he's going to get hurt."

"But Wylie Savage is up to no good!" Wishbone strained against Joe's hold, but it was no use.

"You're coming home with me, boy," Joe said firmly. "I want to make sure you're safe and sound."

"*I'm* not the one who needs protection, Joe. The duck pond does." Wishbone let out a sigh, and waited beside Joe. He had to find a way to get his warning across to his pal.

Chapter Fourteen

Sam lay back against the pillows on her bed later that evening. Somehow, she had managed to do her homework. It was getting quite late, but Sam couldn't sleep until she read more of *Dracula*. As she turned the pages, the story was growing more and more frightening.

The young woman, Lucy, had finally died. Even though her friends had made great attempts to save her, Dracula drank so much of her blood that she couldn't survive. Lucy's coffin was placed inside a tomb. But she didn't stay there for long. Within days, Lucy began to kill because she, too, was now a vampire.

Sam couldn't stand the thought that Lucy had become evil, just like Dracula. Lucy had been so full of joy and goodness. Sam could sympathize with the four men who had loved Lucy. Their cherished friend had now become their enemy.

With a sigh, Sam put the book down. The witch's hat lay on her desk. Next to it were the black cape and the scrap of paper with the phone number on it. The joker's things.

Was the joker like Lucy—no longer a friend?

A knock sounded at Sam's bedroom door. "Come in," she called.

The door opened a crack, and her dad's face appeared. "Are you all right?" he asked. "You seemed really upset after what happened at Oakdale Sports and Games tonight."

Sam gave a half-smile. She had told her dad about the phone call, and scaring Marcus. He realized she was upset and frustrated.

"I guess the practical jokes are really getting to me in a bad way," she admitted. "And some of the pranks have been really mean-spirited. Before, I wouldn't have questioned that people are basically good," she went on. "But now . . ."

"You're beginning to wonder?" her father guessed.

"I don't like to admit it, but I am," Sam said, frowning. "And I'm not the only one. You should have seen the suspicious way kids were looking at one another today while we were working. This isn't much fun anymore. And it's all because someone we know is being mean."

Her dad came all the way into her room and sat down on the edge of her bed. "Are the pranks *meant* to be mean?" he asked.

Sam hugged herself and leaned back against her pillows. "I don't *want* to think so. It's hard to imagine that Amanda could be so vicious. Or Sarah or Curtis. Or even Damont . . ." she said. "But the joker makes his own rules. And you know what else? So far, the joker is winning."

"Don't underestimate yourself, honey," he said. "I happen to know that you've got something special that makes you a very tough person for someone like the joker to beat."

"What's that?" Sam asked.

"The ability to understand others," he said.

Sam didn't see how that made her a strong rival. "But—"

"You have excellent instincts about people, Sam," he went on, before she could voice her question. "You probably know more about the Halloween joker than you realize. That can give you a real edge in figuring out how to deal with the situation. You just need to trust yourself more."

Her father leaned over and kissed her on the forehead.

"You can do it, honey. I know you can." Her dad reached out to give a tug to the ends of her hair. "Good night, Sam," he said. Then he left the room, closing the door behind him.

Sam thought about her father's words. It felt good to know that he believed in her.

Sam glanced down at the cover of *Dracula*. In the book, Dracula was going after a new victim, Jonathan Harker's fiancée, Mina. Jonathan and Professor Van Helsing couldn't stand the thought of watching Mina be destroyed by the vampire, as Lucy had been. Her life was in grave danger!

Professor Van Helsing realized that Dracula would continue to prey on other innocent people forever—unless he was stopped. Van Helsing and Jonathan decided that they would continue fighting and not let Dracula's power spread. They decided to join together and destroy his evil strength. That meant they had to destroy Lucy and Dracula.

One line from the book had made a very strong impression on Sam: "The world seems full of good men—even if there *are* monsters in it. . . ."

Dracula had outsmarted his opponents many times. Yet Professor Van Helsing and Jonathan never gave up believing in themselves and their power to defeat evil. They set off on their monster hunt armed with swords and crucifixes. But their most powerful weapon was the information they had gathered about the vampire. They were ready to use their knowledge of the vampire against him.

That's what I have to do, too, Sam realized. *I need to use what I know to catch the joker.*

Still, the Halloween party was less than twenty-four hours away. That didn't leave her much time at all to act.

"'Morning, Mom," Joe said, as he came into the kitchen Friday morning. "Hi, Wishbone."

Wishbone was bending over his food dish,

gobbling up his kibble. He glanced up at Joe and wagged his tail. Then he turned back to his favorite job of eating.

"'Morning," said Joe's mother. She was drinking coffee while she read the morning paper. Glancing up from it, she smiled at Joe. "Tonight's the big night," she said. "Are you ready for the party?"

Joe shrugged. "I guess so," he said, as he reached for a cereal box and a bowl.

"It sounds like you and Sam and everyone else have worked really hard," his mother commented. "I admire the way you've all gotten the party together in just a few days—even with the joker making it difficult for you."

Joe turned as Wishbone stepped away from his bowl. With a quick look at Joe, the dog ran through his doggie door and out onto the porch. A moment later he was through the back door and in the backyard.

"Oh—that reminds me," Ellen said, watching Wishbone. "Wanda called last night. She's having an exterminator come today. He's going to work on her house to get rid of the ants, inside and outside. The man doing the job says the process is safe. Still, Wanda is concerned about the health of the kids and animals in the neighborhood. We should probably keep Wishbone inside."

"He's not going to like the idea of that," Joe said. He looked through the window, but Wishbone had already trotted out of sight. "I'll bring him in after breakfast."

Joe finished eating his cereal.

After Joe cleared away his dishes, he went out to the backyard. "Wishbone!" he called.

He searched the entire yard. He checked Wanda's flower beds. He even looked into the woods that lined the street opposite their house. No sign of Wishbone. Finally, he gave up and went back inside.

"He's gone, Mom. And I've got to go to school now," Joe said.

"Thanks for looking, Joe. Today's my day off. I'll keep an eye out for him. With luck, he'll return shortly."

Joe nodded. "Thanks, Mom," he said as he grabbed his backpack.

Considering how things are going, Joe thought, *I don't think we can count on having luck on our side.*

Chapter Fifteen

Sam walked down the first-floor hallway of Sequoyah Middle School on Friday morning. Her backpack was slung over her shoulder, and the copy of *Dracula* was in her jacket pocket. As Sam fingered the smooth cover, she was more determined than ever to unmask the Halloween joker.

In *Dracula,* the vampire hunt was heating up. Sam almost felt as if she were right there with Professor Van Helsing and Jonathan. It had taken all their bravery to enter the run-down old house where Dracula was staying. The house gave off a nauseating smell of old blood. The air seemed infected with pain and death. Even when faced with swarms of mice and a pack of howling dogs, the vampire hunters had stuck to their task. Sam had expected Count Dracula to leap from a dark corner at any time.

Sam had hoped that the characters would close in on Dracula. But he had managed to escape them once again. Now he was on a ship sailing from England to a port near his home in Transylvania. Sam had left off her reading at the point where the vampire hunters were heading overland for the same port. If they could reach the port ahead of Dracula, they felt sure that they could trap and destroy him.

Sam felt as if she, too, were in a race against time. She had to find and expose the joker before the Halloween party at Oakdale Sports & Games later that night.

Sam glanced down the row of lockers that lined the hallway. Dozens of kids were taking off their jackets and getting together their books for their classes. But Sam was looking for one girl in particular.

"Amanda!" Sam ran forward as she caught sight of Amanda. The other girl was standing in front of her locker, about halfway down the hall.

"Hi, Sam. What's up?" she said.

"*This* is." Sam unzipped her backpack and pulled out the witch's hat that Wishbone had found the night before. "Doesn't it belong to you?"

Amanda's eyes flickered with an emotion Sam couldn't quite read. Guilt? Fear? Sam wasn't sure.

When Amanda didn't answer her question, Sam said, "The joker struck again last night. Whoever it was wore this hat."

"Really?" Amanda asked, raising an eyebrow.

"Look, I know you're disappointed that your idea was not accepted," Sam said. "But, still, that's no reason to—"

"You still think *I'm* the joker?" Amanda interrupted. She shook her head firmly. "You're way off base, Sam."

"*Am* I?" Sam asked. Sam did not have absolute proof that Amanda was the joker. It was just a gut feeling.

"I don't have to explain myself to you," Amanda said.

But Sam wasn't going to let Amanda off the hook so easily. "You've been acting like you're the joker's biggest fan, Amanda," Sam said. "I saw you poking around Oakdale Sports and Games yesterday. And then, right after that, we found *your* witch's hat right where the joker appeared again. I know you're up to something."

Amanda's self-confident smile faded. She did not say anything at first. At last, the girl took a deep breath and said, "I *did* have a reason for being at the store yesterday."

Sam felt a twinge of excitement. Finally, she was getting somewhere!

"But, I'm *not* the Halloween joker," Amanda said flatly.

"Huh?" Sam blinked at Amanda in surprise.

Amanda frowned down at the floor. Sam had the feeling the girl was deciding something. "It's a surprise," Amanda said. "For the party tonight."

"What *kind* of surprise?" she asked. "Not the kind that involves pulling off another practical joke, I hope."

"I am *not* the joker," Amanda said firmly. "If I was, I would never have told you what I just did."

Sam looked at Amanda carefully, searching for any sign that she might be hiding the truth. But Amanda's face and voice were sincere.

She is a good actress, Sam reminded herself. *Can I really trust her?*

"Thanks for coming with me to talk to David again," Sam told Joe that afternoon after school. "We have to join together if we're going to catch the joker."

Joe kept his hands in his jacket pockets as he and Sam walked toward David's house. "It's a good idea. We need as much help as we can get."

The cold autumn wind felt energizing. Joe felt as if it were driving him and Sam on an important mission.

"Anyway, Dracula's castle is just about ready, and the party is still a few hours away," Sam said. "We may as well make the most of the time we have left before the party starts."

They had spent the last hour and a half with the other volunteers at Oakdale Sports & Games. They had made final adjustments to the lighting. They had also checked to make sure that each area of the castle worked the way it was supposed to.

"It was pretty cool, seeing the castle come together," Joe said, as he and Sam turned onto the wooded street where he and David lived. "The flapping bats and swooping vampires and Dracula popping out of his coffin . . . They're all great. And the sound effects of the howling wolves are really convincing."

"I just hope the only tricks that happen tonight are the ones we planned," Sam said, frowning.

Joe turned as he suddenly saw the front door to his house open. His mother appeared in the doorway. "Joe?" she called out. "Have you seen Wishbone?"

"No," he answered.

Seeing the concerned expression on his mom's face, Joe began to worry. He had forgotten all about the exterminator. He turned to look at Wanda's house. A white truck was just pulling out of her driveway.

"'Wylie Savage—Pest Control.'" Joe frowned as he read aloud the words on the truck door. "Mom, you don't think . . ."

"I've been keeping an eye on Wanda's house all day," his mother said. "I'm almost positive Wishbone hasn't been over there. But I don't know where he *has* been. I put out some ginger snaps for him an hour ago. They're still there."

Sam raised an eyebrow at Joe. "Wishbone

usually has an unbelievable sense of radar when it comes to snacks. I wonder where he is."

"Sam and I have to stop by to see David," Joe told his mom. "I'll look for Wishbone after that. But he's probably fine."

Still, as Joe and Sam continued toward David's house, he found himself concerned about Wishbone, too.

Where *was* he?

Chapter Sixteen

"Out of the way, everyone! Canine patrol coming through!" Wishbone barked at some birds that were pecking at seeds next to the duck pond Friday afternoon. As they scattered, Wishbone continued to trot along the water's edge. "Sorry, guys, can't stop to chase you. I'm busy guarding the edge of the pond. One dog, prepared to fight off crime and evil, and keep the pond safe for feathered and furred creatures everywhere."

Wishbone had been at his patrol duty all day. Three times, he'd checked out the duck pond, searching for possible trouble. So far, all was calm.

"Wylie Savage is going to be in for big trouble if he shows up. Beneath this handsome, furred exterior lies the heart of a warrior!"

As the afternoon light began to fade, Wishbone

gazed at the plastic containers Wylie had dumped in the pond before. Somehow they got trapped in the thick mud nearby. Wishbone wished there were some way he could make them disappear altogether.

A low, rumbling noise echoed in Wishbone's ears. "Snack time," he said. His stomach always growled at that time of day. Wishbone pictured ginger snaps, just waiting for him in his dish, and his mouth started to water. "I always say, never do battle on an empty stomach. . . ." He was prepared to fight.

Wishbone cocked his head to one side as *another* rumbling noise caught his attention. This time it *wasn't* coming from his stomach. It was coming from the very same path the bug man had used the last time he had driven up to dump cans in the pond. Wishbone wasn't surprised when he spotted Wylie Savage's white truck bumping down the path toward the pond.

When Wishbone looked at the back of the truck, his fur stood on end. He saw several more plastic cans!

"Okay, buster! Empty stomach or not . . . you've met your match!" Wishbone trotted toward the truck as it turned off the path. Then he yelped and jumped back. "Hey! Not so close! I'd like to keep *all* four paws, thank you!"

The truck had swerved on the muddy tracks, coming within half a foot of Wishbone. As Wishbone gazed up at the truck, he reconsidered his plan. *Looks like I'm going to need reinforcements,* he thought, backing away.

Wishbone felt his tail brush against some soggy cattails at the edge of the pond. The cattails smelled of the milky chemical that still clouded the water. Their stalks were covered with this same jelly-like material.

"Hmm . . ." Wishbone closed his mouth around the stalks, being careful not to touch the bad spots. *Maybe there's a way to get my message across to Joe, after all. . . .*

Sam and Joe walked up David's driveway. "There he is," she said.

The door to David's garage workroom was open. David was inside, standing next to something large and boxy. The garage light reflected off sections of mirror that were set up in a semicircle. Sam didn't have a chance to see more than that, though. As soon as David saw her and Joe approaching, he grabbed a big cloth and threw it over his invention.

"We need to talk, David," Sam said.

"Can't it wait?" David frowned, glancing back at his surprise. "The party is just a few hours away, and I'm still doing some fine-tuning."

Sam wished that David would be more open and helpful. But she reminded herself that he had been completely occupied with his surprise. Maybe he didn't fully understand how serious the practical jokes were becoming.

"You know, some people are convinced that *you're* the Halloween joker, David," Joe told his good friend.

"You're not talking about the tape recording of the scream again, are you?" David said, glancing from Sam to Joe. "I already explained about that."

"Joe and I believe you," Sam said. "But you have to admit, it looks suspicious. The dry ice *and* the scream that were used to scare Sarah came from right here," Sam continued, pointing around David's workshop.

Joe leaned back against one of the garage walls. "Plus, the joker called Sam at Miss Gilmore's on Wednesday afternoon, to warn her about the stink bomb," he said. "You were one of the few people who knew she was there. That makes you an even bigger suspect in a lot of people's eyes—especially Sarah's."

"David, if we're going to figure out who the real joker is, we need your help," Sam added.

David glanced at the bulky object that was covered by the dropcloth. "I didn't realize . . ." Then he turned to them with a sincere smile and said, "Count me in. What can I do to help?"

Sam gave a deep sigh of relief. With David helping her and Joe, they would be that much more powerful a force against the joker. "If Professor Van Helsing and a handful of friends can make the most evil vampire of all time go running scared, the three of us should be able to catch the Halloween joker."

"Professor Van Helsing?" David asked, raising an eyebrow at her.

"Are we talking about *Dracula* now?" Joe added.

"Good guess," Sam said, laughing.

She gave a quick rundown of what had happened in the story since she had last spoken about it. When she described the hunt that Professor Van Helsing and Jonathan had set out on, Joe let out a whistle.

"A monster hunt, huh?" he said. "That sounds cool."

"I feel like that's what we're doing, too," Sam pointed out. "The joker is smart and sneaky. We're going to have to be even smarter. And that means finding out everything we can."

Sam took a deep breath and turned to David.

"I think we should start with you," Sam continued. "The joker took the tape recording and the dry ice from you. You might know more than you think."

"Maybe you'd better tell us what you were doing at the times of the pranks," Joe suggested. "And try to think about anything unusual that you remember noticing."

Sam and Joe went down the list of practical jokes: the skeleton prank that scared Joe and Wishbone on Tuesday, as well as the recorded scream and smashed pumpkin and dry-ice fog outside Sarah's house that same night. Then there was the stink bomb the joker threw at Hank on Wednesday. And on Thursday, there was the scare

Sam had received inside Dracula's tomb, and the chase behind Oakdale Sports & Games.

David listened, deep in thought. When Sam and Joe were finished running down their list of the joker's attacks, David gave another tap to the bulk that was covered by the dropcloth. "I've been working on this practically every moment I wasn't in school," he said. "I was right here when every single one of those practical jokes was pulled."

David looked over at Sam and Joe, shaking his head.

"It's amazing," he added. "Whoever it is, is going all out to leave a big black mark on this Halloween celebration."

"I agree," Sam said. "The joker is definitely enjoying all the attention the pranks are getting. I can hear it in the joker's voice when I get those phone calls right before the pranks happen."

"When I did my vampire routine at Oakdale Sports and Games, it was kind of cool," David said thoughtfully. "But once was definitely enough. It wouldn't be fun for me if I thought people were really scared."

"That's the difference between you and the joker," Joe said. "When the joker pulls a stunt, it's always at someone *else's* expense."

David looked at Sam and said, "And it's like

the practical jokes are a big challenge between the joker and you. I guess I was busy thinking about making my *own* mark this Halloween."

"It's all right," Sam said.

She really meant it. She was glad David was on her side.

"You know, my dad was right," Sam went on. "He told me we probably knew more about the joker than we realized. I think we just came up with a pretty good profile, don't you, guys?"

"Well," Joe said, "we're looking for someone who likes to be the center of attention . . . someone who pits himself—or herself—against other people . . ."

"And someone who enjoys scaring other people," David finished. "The joker is not a nice person."

Sam frowned. "That's what's been bothering me," she admitted. "So far, the likeliest suspects are Damont, Curtis, and Amanda," she said. "Maybe even Sarah. Every one of them had the opportunity to pull most, if not all, of the practical jokes. But I just can't imagine that any of them could be that mean."

Joe and David looked at each other. Then David shrugged and said, "What other clues do you have?"

"Well, we've got the hat to a witch's costume,"

Sam told him. "That points to Amanda. Then there's the black cape and phone number. . . ." She told David where and when they had found each of those pieces of evidence. "I've dialed the number a few times, but I never get an answer."

"It can't hurt to call it again. Do you have the number with you?" David asked.

"Yes—right here." Sam smiled and pointed to her head. "I've stared at it so often, I know it by heart."

David went inside his house and then came back into the garage with a portable phone. He handed the phone to Sam and she dialed the number.

"Please don't get your hopes up," she said, as she heard ringing over the line. "So far no one has ever—"

Sam broke off talking as a voice came over the line: "Hello?"

"Yes! Hi!" Sam gave David and Joe a quick thumb's-up sign. Then she spoke into the mouthpiece. "Who is this?"

"This is a pay phone. If you don't know who you're calling, I can't help you," said the person at the other end of the line. It was a boy's voice. Sam didn't recognize it, but whoever it was sounded annoyed.

"Who is this?" Sam asked again.

"Look, if you're trying to find the guy in the orange shirt, he took off," the boy said. "Can you try again later? I'm waiting for my brother to call me back."

Sam frowned, trying to make sense of what the boy was saying. "*What* boy in the orange shirt?" she asked.

"The one who kept trying to get me off the phone so *he* could use it. But I told him, and I'm telling you . . . I'm waiting for my brother to call back, so please stop bothering me!"

Sam wasn't sure what to make of the caller. But she couldn't just hang up. "Wait!" she said. "Where is the pay phone you're using?"

"If you don't know, that's not my problem," the boy said.

"Just tell me where you are," Sam urged. "Please?"

She could hear the sigh of frustration the boy let out. "Oak Street, right outside Rosie's Rendezvous. Satisfied?" he said.

Sam smiled to herself. "Thanks," she said into the phone. "'Bye."

"What was *that* all about?" Joe asked after Sam had hung up.

"I'm not sure," Sam said. As she repeated

what the boy had told her, she still didn't know what to make of the phone call.

"Do you think the boy you talked to is involved with the practical jokes?" David asked when she was done.

Sam shrugged. "The voice was muffled but still seemed different from the joker's," she said. "Higher, and younger-sounding. I think he really *was* just waiting for his brother to call, like he said."

"What about the boy with the orange shirt?" Joe asked.

"That could be anyone. It's a pay phone, after all," Sam said. "But at least we found out where the pay phone is."

"Outside Rosie's Rendezvous, huh?" David said. He frowned, crossing his arms over his chest. "That's right down the street from Oakdale Sports and Games."

"Yes," said Joe. "But I still don't understand how the joker could—" He broke off, looking out the garage door. "Wishbone? Is that you, boy?"

Sam heard the familiar jangle of Wishbone's dog tags a second before he appeared at the garage. His paws were wet and covered with mud. She saw the cattails that Wishbone held in his muzzle. "I can guess where you've been,

Wishbone. How's everything over at the duck pond?"

"I sure am glad to see you," Joe said. As Wishbone trotted over to him, Joe bent down to pet him. "I hope you stayed away from Miss Gilmore's house. The exterminator—" Joe broke off talking for a moment. "There's that gross chemical smell again," he said. "What do you keep getting yourself into, Wishbone?"

Sam smelled it, too. A sharp odor stung her nose. As she looked more closely, she saw some clear, jelly-like material on the stalks of the cattails. "What *is* that?" she wondered aloud.

Wishbone let the cattails drop to the garage floor. He sniffed at the cattails. Then he jumped around Joe's feet, barking.

Sam touched some of the slimy, clear substance. Then she winced at the stinging smell. "This is some kind of chemical, guys. And it's not good! How did it get on the cattails?"

Wishbone let out another loud bark. He took a few steps back toward the driveway. Then he stopped and barked some more.

"What is it, boy?" Joe frowned. Then he turned to Sam and David.

Sam didn't like the look or feel or smell of the chemical that was on the cattails. "If that chemical is on these cattails, then there's probably more of it over at the duck pond. In the town of Oakdale, you can only find cattails by the pond," she said. "We've got to do something!"

Wishbone let out another bark, then ran farther down the driveway. "I think he wants us to follow him," Joe said.

"Shouldn't we tell someone about this?" asked David.

"Miss Gilmore is a very active member of the tree-preservation society. She knows all about plants and stuff like that. I'll show these to her," Sam said. She picked up the cattails and headed outside. "You two go with Wishbone. I'll check to be sure Miss Gilmore's at home. If she is, we'll meet you at the duck pond as soon as we can!"

Chapter Seventeen

"Yes! You people are finally starting to get my message. And not a moment too soon! Now, follow the clever dog, folks. . . ." Wishbone kicked up his paws and ran down David's driveway. He headed straight for Jackson Park.

"Slow down, Wishbone!" Joe called out.

"Sorry, Joe. No can do. This is a red-alert emergency!" Wishbone kept running. He slowed down only when Joe and David lagged out of sight behind him. Before long, the boys settled into a steady rhythm, jogging behind Wishbone.

"You guys are pretty fast, considering you've got only two legs each." Wishbone looked back to see Joe and David run into Jackson Park right behind him. He barked. Then he took off down the path that led to the duck pond.

"What is Wishbone so worked up about?" David asked breathlessly. "I feel as if we're training for a marathon."

"Oh, this is a contest, all right . . ." Wishbone's paws crunched over dried leaves as he crossed the ditch, then began to run up the rise right in front of the pond. "It's a fight between good and evil. We've got to get to the pond before that bug killer gets away with dumping more cans in *my* pond!"

Wishbone's ears perked up as he heard the low rumble of the truck motor.

"There's the monster now! After him!"

Barking, Wishbone leaped over the top of the rise. The first thing he saw was the white bulk of the bug man's truck, next to the pond. Then he spotted Wylie Savage himself. The man was just getting into his truck. . . .

"What's that truck doing over there?" Joe's voice spoke up behind Wishbone. He sounded winded, and concerned. "Cars and trucks aren't allowed anywhere in the park."

"This guy doesn't play by the rules. But there's no time to explain. Come on!" Wishbone cried.

The dog ran as fast as his four legs would carry him. He barked loudly at Wylie Savage as he went.

"I'm tough, I'm fast, and this time I'm *not* going to let you get away!"

Joe and David continued right behind the dog. Wishbone heard their sneakers pounding over the earth, crunching down on dried leaves and sticks.

"What . . . ?" Wylie Savage paused with his truck door half open. Even in the shadowy light of dusk, Wishbone saw the cold glint in the man's eyes as he looked toward them.

Pepper was sitting on the seat next to Wylie. He started to bark when he heard Wishbone.

"Shut up, Pepper!" Wylie commanded. The black dog fell silent. Wylie slammed his door shut. The truck lights blinked on, and Wylie started to shift the truck into reverse gear.

"Not this time . . ." Wishbone ran behind the truck, blocking its way. Within seconds, Joe and David had joined him there.

"What's going on?" Wylie leaned out the truck window, glaring at Wishbone, Joe, and David. "Get out of my way!" he threatened.

"Not until we find out what's going on here," Joe said.

Wishbone was proud of the way his buddy stood his ground. "Way to go, Joe!"

Joe and David looked around with confused

expressions. Wishbone guessed they were having trouble seeing everything clearly in the darkening evening.

"Over here!" Wishbone ran to the edge of the pond, where the plastic containers sat in the mud. The front lights of the truck lit up the plastic rims of several new containers in the isolated pool near the bushes.

"Look!" David said with excitement, pointing at the containers.

Wishbone saw Joe glance from the containers to Wylie Savage's truck. "Pest control, huh?" Joe murmured. He crinkled up his nose and sniffed the air. "*That's* the chemical I've been smelling on Wishbone! This must be where he got it on himself. . . ." Joe turned to Wylie Savage with a look of shock. "You've been dumping pesticides in the duck pond!"

"Bingo!" Wishbone barked out his approval. "Not bad for someone untrained in the canine arts of searching and sniffing."

Wylie got out of the truck. Still frowning, he walked slowly toward Joe and David. "I don't know what you boys are talking about," Wylie said. "I'm just a man trying to make an honest living."

Wishbone ran over and stood so that he was between Wylie and Joe and David. "That's close enough, buster! They don't call me Guard Dog for nothing!"

Wylie Savage looked down at Wishbone and gave a bitter laugh. "You're just kids," he said. "If you go to the police, it'll be your word against mine. But, trust me, it won't ever come to that."

Suddenly, Pepper jumped out of the truck through the open doorway. He cocked his head to one side, gazing uncertainly at Wishbone.

"Hi, there!" Wishbone gave the dog a big smile. "Remember me? I'm Wishbone."

Wishbone couldn't tell whether Pepper remembered him or not. The black dog danced nervously from paw to paw, glancing up at Wylie.

The dog's ears went back. A low growl rumbled in his throat. He crouched down, as if he were about to leap.

"Wait a minute! We were starting to become friends, remember? I even offered you one of my favorite doggie treats a few days ago." Wishbone took a tentative step toward Pepper.

The other dog hesitated.

Wishbone heard a noise behind him. He turned to see Wanda Gilmore and Sam running around the edge of the pond toward them.

"What's going on here?" Wanda aimed a very

CAUTION

serious look at Wylie Savage—then blinked in surprise. "Wylie? What are you doing here? Don't you know trucks aren't allowed in the park?"

"That's the least of his crimes, Wanda!" Wishbone barked.

Wanda's gaze swept over the duck pond. When she saw the plastic containers, her eyes went wide with shock and anger. "If this is what I think it is," she said, turning to Wylie, "you're in big trouble."

Wishbone's tail wagged triumphantly as he trotted over to the man. "You're busted!"

"Wow! I can't believe Mr. Savage was dumping pesticides in the duck pond," Joe said. It was an hour later, and he, Sam, David, and Wishbone were walking out of the Oakdale police station. They had just finished giving a statement to the police about what they had witnessed at the duck pond.

Wanda had called the police just before she left for Jackson Park. After she saw the cattail, she suspected what was going on. After Officer Krulla had seen what Wylie had done to the duck pond, the police officer had brought him in to arrest him. Wanda, Joe, Sam, David, and Wishbone had gone along to tell all they could about the dumping. Wanda was still at the police station, answering questions. But Sam, Joe, and David had had to leave so they could get ready for the Halloween party at Oakdale Sports & Games. Wishbone went with the kids.

As they walked down Oak Street, Joe shook his head in amazement. For the last few days, he had been worrying about what prank the joker might pull next. But after their run-in with Wylie Savage, Joe knew that there were even more terrible things happening in Oakdale than he had suspected.

Joe began to wonder what *else* would go wrong.

"If Wishbone hadn't brought those cattails to show us," Sam said as she walked next to Joe, "Mr. Wylie might have gotten away with his crime!"

Joe reached down to scratch the terrier behind the ears. "I'm really proud of you, Wishbone," he said. "I sure am glad you weren't hurt, boy. Those chemicals are dangerous."

"Officer Krulla told me it was a good thing the plastic containers had been dumped in an isolated pool," David said. "The water there is very still, so the chemicals mostly settled right in one area on the bottom. The rest of the pond wasn't affected. And Wanda said the conservation society can clean up the pool that *was* polluted. She's almost sure there won't be any long-term damage."

"What an awful thing to do," Sam said, frowning. "Mr. Savage was ruining a beautiful place, just to save a little money. If he had kept on dumping chemicals in the duck pond, it might have become completely unsafe."

Wishbone barked up at Sam, as if to show he agreed with her. Joe had to agree, too. They had learned from the police officer that because pesticides were so poisonous, Wylie was required to get rid of them in a special waste-dumping site. That cost money—money that Wylie simply hadn't been willing to spend.

"I'm sure that now he regrets what he did," David said. "Officer Krulla made it clear that even if Mr. Savage doesn't go to jail, he'll have to pay a big fine."

As they approached Oakdale Sports & Games, they saw that the store was brightly lit. Out front, the skeleton, bat, obstacles, and vampire of the Transylvania miniature-golf course glowed in the yellow light. Travis was just setting up a huge cardboard sign next to the store's entrance. It was cut out in the shape of Dracula, and was painted with the caped image of the vampire. Ghoulish white letters were painted across the cape:

DRACULA'S CASTLE OF DOOM
Enter at Your Own Risk

"We'd better get home so we can dress in our costumes," Joe said, checking his watch.

"No kidding," Sam agreed. "The party starts in just an hour!"

As they picked up their pace, Joe tried to think ahead. He, Sam, and most of the other volunteers were dressing as vampires for the party. It would take him only a few minutes to put on his dark clothes and cape. Then all he had to do was slick back his hair and—

"Look. Isn't that Curtis?" Sam's voice broke into Joe's thoughts.

Curtis was standing on the sidewalk outside Rosie's Rendezvous, looking bored. Joe didn't think anything special of it—until he noticed Curtis's shirt.

"Sam, didn't that kid from the pay phone tell you that someone wearing an *orange* shirt was trying to keep the phone free?" Joe asked.

Sam gave a knowing nod. "Curtis is wearing orange. *And* he's standing right next to the same pay phone the kid was using," she said.

"So, the phone number you found in the fireman's locker is for *this* pay phone. And now we find Curtis waiting there," David said. His eyes narrowed as he gazed at Curtis a second time. "Do you see what he's holding?"

Joe hadn't noticed the bulging plastic bag that dangled from Curtis's hand. "Come on," Joe said. "Let's go find out what he's up to."

Curtis didn't see them until they were just a few yards away. He backed up slightly, and his grip tightened around the plastic bag.

"Hi, Curtis," Sam said. "Shouldn't you be getting ready to help out at the Halloween party?"

Joe noticed the nervous look in Curtis's eyes as they flickered from him, to Sam, to David. "I . . . uh . . . I'll be there, don't worry," Curtis said.

I'll bet, thought Joe. *But you probably won't be helping. . . .*

"What do you have in there?" Joe asked the other boy, nodding at the bag in Curtis's hand.

"Nothing!" Curtis took another step back.

David gave him a smooth smile and said, "If it's stuff for the party, we'll be glad to take it over there for you—you know, since it looks like you're running late and all."

"No way," Curtis said, shifting the bag so that it was behind him. "I don't have to . . . Hey! Get away from there, Wishbone!"

Wishbone had trotted over to Curtis. He began to sniff at the bag. Curtis tried to pull it away. But Wishbone's teeth had already closed around one of the plastic ties. As Curtis yanked, the plastic ripped, and a pile of things clattered to the sidewalk.

"Oh, no!" Curtis dropped to his knees. He tried to scoop up the items, but he wasn't fast enough. Joe knelt down and grabbed a plastic bag. It was filled with small balls of different colors.

"'Exploding caps,'" he said, reading the label. He frowned and held out the bag for Sam and David to see. "They make a loud popping noise when you throw them down and they hit the ground."

"Look at these," David added. He held up a small blue canister. "Wacky string. It's that spaghetti-like foam stuff you can spray all over people."

Sam sifted through the other items that lay on the sidewalk. "Here's more stink bombs, flash powder . . ." She picked up a handful of the stuff and held it out to Curtis. "What were you going to use this for?" she asked.

Curtis backed slowly away from them. He didn't answer Sam's question. One look at his guilty face, though, and Joe knew the answer.

Joe reached out and grabbed Curtis's arm. Then he turned to Sam and David and said, "It looks as if we've found the Halloween joker, guys."

Chapter Eighteen

"Five minutes until we open the door," Travis Del Rio said a short while later. "Is everything ready?"

Sam gave a careful look around Oakdale Sports & Games and responded, "Let me quickly check around one more time." Just forty-five minutes had passed since she, Joe, David, and Wishbone had caught the joker, Curtis, with his bag of tricks. They had taken away all the items, and now Curtis was not being permitted to come to the party. Word spread quickly that the joker had been caught.

Sam wasn't sure how she had managed to run home, get into her vampire costume, and then make it back to Oakdale Sports & Games in time for the beginning of the party. Somehow, she had done it. Now, as she glanced around, she had to admit that Dracula's castle looked very real.

The painted castle loomed over a rocky cliff against one wall. Bats fluttered from their strings next to the fire pole. Sam could see Hank in his Dracula costume at the top of the pole, waiting to swoop down on unsuspecting partygoers. The central graveyard—with its crumbling headstones, fake trees, and staring, yellow-eyed wolves—created the exact creepy mood Sam had planned.

Dracula's tomb, in the back corner under the stairs, looked dark and scary. Screens painted with haunting, creepy landscapes separated the different areas of the castle. Various games were scattered throughout.

Volunteers dressed in costumes were positioned around the store to help guide young kids from place to place. Sam liked the way the colored lights threw an eerie, unreal glow over everything. The pre-recorded sounds of howling made the atmosphere even spookier.

As Sam gazed at the scene, she felt jumpy, uncomfortable. *We've already caught the joker,* she reminded herself. *I must just have nervous butterflies, the way some actors do before they go onstage in a play.*

"I *guess* we're ready." Sam turned to Travis

with a doubtful smile. "Even Wishbone is here to help out."

She pointed toward the central graveyard. Wishbone trotted among the fake gravestones, stopping every now and then to smell a cardboard wolf or papier-mâché gravestone. "All we have to do is put David's surprise in place," Sam added.

David and his father had just arrived with a large bundle that was protected by cardboard on all sides. As Sam and Joe helped to roll it in on a cart, David glanced around curiously. "Everything looks fantastic," he said.

"David, show us your surprise," Joe said. "You can't keep us in suspense any longer. We've already waited long enough."

Sam directed the group to an open area at one end of the central graveyard. She, Joe, and David eased the heavy object off the cart. Sam held her breath as David untaped the cardboard panels. When he pulled the panels away, Sam's mouth dropped open.

"Wow! . . ." was all she could say.

"It's a game," David explained. "It's like a bean-bag toss . . . but with my own special design."

David's game consisted of half a dozen brightly painted targets set in a half-circle. Each target was painted with a different geometric design. One held a black-and-white swirl that made Sam feel dizzy when she looked at it. Another showed a court jester costumed with red and purple diamonds. Yet another one had dogs chasing one another's tails around a bright red circle. Five mirrored panels had been set in between the targets at different angles. As Sam looked at them, she saw endless reflections of herself and the targets. The effect was dizzying—and a little disturbing.

"Cool," Joe said, staring at the game. "How does it work?"

David picked up a handful of bean bags from a bin he had made in the center of the semicircle. He handed one to Joe and one to Sam.

Looking down at her bean bag, Sam saw that David had attached bat wings to it and drawn beady bat's eyes.

"Use these to hit the targets," David told them.

Sam chose the target with the black-and-white swirl. But with so many reflected images staring back at her, it was hard to aim. "Here I go," she said.

She took aim and threw, but her bean bag struck one of the mirrors instead of the target.

"This isn't easy," she said, smiling at David.

Picking up a second bean-bag bat, Sam took aim again. This time, the bat struck the target.

Sam was surprised when a ghoulish face appeared from behind the target. It let out a terrifying—and very familiar—shrieking laugh.

"So, *that's* why you made the recording," Sam said, chuckling.

Joe tried the next target. He aimed for the jester. When he struck it, a mechanical vampire jumped from its coffin. "Not bad," he said.

Some other volunteers gathered around to play the game. One of them hit another target, and a handful of candy corn slid down a ramp and into a small cup. The girl reached for the candy, but Wishbone was faster. Sam laughed as the terrier gobbled up most of the candy corn, his tail wagging with joy.

"You'll have to wait your turn, boy," Joe said. He grabbed Wishbone's collar and pulled him away from the rest of the candy.

"So, *this* is the surprise you've been working on, huh, David?" Sarah said, as she stepped over to the game. She was wearing an old-fashioned dress with a flowing skirt. As Sarah turned to David, Sam saw two blood-red gashes on Sarah's neck. Looking closer, Sam could see that the marks were just made with lipstick.

"I guess I was wrong about you, David," Sarah said. "But I want to know something. Did Curtis tell you how he got the recorded scream and the dry ice from your garage workshop?"

"Not yet. We didn't have time to get the full story," David said. "I guess we'll find out when we talk to him again after the party is over."

"Who cares *how* he got them?" said another boy. "What's important is that Curtis was caught."

Sam glanced around at the other volunteers. For the first time in days, they looked happy and excited. Still, Sam had a hard time shaking off her own nervous jitters. Sarah's question made Sam realize that they *hadn't* had a chance to learn all the details of how Curtis had pulled the practical jokes. Sam didn't like to leave loose ends hanging. But she didn't have any choice at the moment.

"Okay, everyone, find your places." Travis clapped his hands and stepped over to the store entrance. "It's party time!"

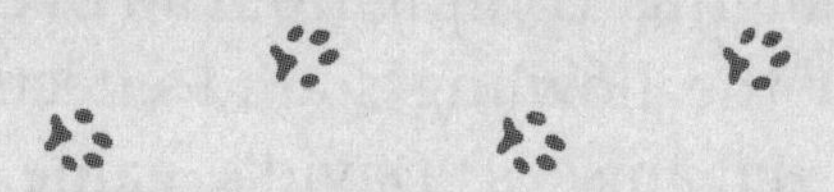

Sam ran for Dracula's tomb. Her job was to operate the coffin that had been set up inside the tomb. The coffin was just big enough for Sam to lie inside it. A rope had been tied to the coffin lid and was looped through a pulley. When a visitor pulled the rope, the lid would open.

Sam quickly climbed inside. She lay perfectly still, her arms crossed over her chest. Before long, she heard giggles as some children entered the tomb. Sam didn't move. She heard the kids' cries of excitement as they pulled the rope and opened the coffin. When Sam was sure the kids had seen her, she sat up right away. She opened her mouth to show her long, fake fangs. Talking in as deep a voice as she could, she said threateningly, "I vant to suck your blood!"

When the kids saw Sam, two boys in cowboy costumes and a girl wearing a ghost costume stood frozen. Then they leaped back, grabbing one another.

"A vampire!" one of them shouted.

Then they ran from the tomb, shrieking with glee.

Sam couldn't help laughing. She could hear

gasps and laughter coming from all over the store. Along with the howling sound effects were the rings and screams of David's game. Sam was pleased with what she heard. It sounded as if the castle was scary—but not *too* scary.

"Oops!" Sam barely had time to close the coffin lid and lie down again before the next visitors arrived. But instead of childlike giggles and laughs, Sam heard David's voice.

"Sam?" he said.

The coffin lid opened. Sam saw David standing there in his vampire costume. "Travis says there's a phone call for you. It's something about your dad. I'll take over here until you come back."

Sam frowned as she climbed out of the coffin.

"My dad? Why would he be calling?" she wondered aloud.

David shrugged. As he climbed into the coffin, Sam went to the phone on the counter next to the cash register. "Hello?" she said into the mouthpiece. "Dad, is everything all right?"

"That was just a trick to get you to the phone, Sam. You know who this really is, don't you?"

The voice that spoke wasn't her father's. It was low and muffled—and it made Sam shiver from head to toe.

It was the Halloween joker.

How could this be happening! a voice screamed out in Sam's mind. She had let herself think that everything was all right. She had ignored the leftover doubts she had.

"Curtis? Why are you calling?" Sam said. She tried to sound brave. But the teasing tone in the joker's voice made her feel suddenly unsure. "You've been told you couldn't attend the party, remember? So there's no way you can pull any more tricks."

"You trapped the wrong joker, Sam," the low, threatening voice said over the line. "The real joker is coming for you. And I'm closer than you think."

The joker's voice was still muffled, but Sam heard bits of noise in the background: a faint wail, the sounds of howling wolves, and laughing children.

"You're right here at the party!" Sam gasped. She suddenly felt as if there wasn't enough air for her to catch her breath.

"You are clever," the joker told her. "By the way, you won't have to look far to find the target of tonight's special event. You're it, Sam."

Sam was shocked. The line went dead. Her eyes scanned over the glowing wolves' eyes, the creepy-looking cave that had been built around the basketball hoop, and the red and blue and green lights that made the costumes and scenery look eerie.

The joker was right out there . . . somewhere . . .

"Where *are* you?" she said sharply. "*Who* are you?"

Suddenly, the lights in the store went out. Screams of delight rang out through the velvety blackness. The kids surely thought this was a planned part of the Halloween party. But Sam knew better.

The Halloween joker was coming to get her.

Chapter Nineteen

Sam felt panic rise up inside her.

She tried to think of what Professor Van Helsing would do if he were in her place. He, Jonathan, and the others had had their share of surprises, too.

The vampire hunters had arrived at a port town near Transylvania. That was where the ship carrying Dracula was scheduled to land. Yet, once again, the vampire had fooled them. Just when Van Helsing thought he had Dracula trapped, he found out he didn't. It was what had happened to Sam.

In the book, Van Helsing and Jonathan guessed that Count Dracula was making his way to his castle at top speed. They realized that once in the castle, Count Dracula would be safe. The vampire hunters' only chance was to catch up with Dracula along the way. They followed bravely, determined to win. . . .

"Boo!" a voice cried out. "I've been waiting for you."

Sam almost jumped out of her skin as a shadowy figure leaped out from behind a screen a few feet away. She recognized the joker's voice. Sam saw the green glimmer of glow-in-the-dark fangs. Then the joker quickly disappeared behind the screen.

Sam closed her eyes and fought back a shiver. She wished she could call out to Joe and David. She was sure that together, they could catch the joker. But she didn't want to scare everyone else.

You can catch the joker yourself, she thought.

Taking a deep breath, Sam tiptoed over to the screen where she had seen the joker. She made a sudden leap to the other side of the screen. But the joker was no longer there.

Slowly, Sam moved forward. Up ahead was the fire pole. Hank was guiding some children away from it. . . .

Sam jumped a second time as someone tapped her from behind. "Gotcha!" the joker's deep voice said, right in her ear.

Sam whirled around with a gasp. The joker

had already ducked back behind a ring-toss game. Sam heard his creepy laugh. Suddenly, she felt more angry than scared.

"I have *had* it!" she said.

In her mind, she pictured the layout of Dracula's castle. She knew every inch of it by heart. But the joker also seemed to know his or her way around, too. When Sam circled around the ring-toss game, the joker had once again disappeared.

Up ahead were the glowing yellow eyes of the wolves. Sam crept toward them, then ducked behind David's game. As she peeked around the side of the game, she caught sight of a dark silhouette squatting behind a gravestone. Was it the joker? Sam didn't see a cape. As the silhouette moved, Sam caught sight of glowing green fangs.

"Yes!" she whispered.

She moved slowly closer to the joker, hiding behind gravestones and wolves. Out of the corner of her eye, Sam saw shadowy shapes of kids in costume. The lights were still out. She heard volunteers asking one another what was going on. Sam tried to tune them out and keep her attention aimed on the joker.

Okay, she thought. *Just a few more yards. . . .*

Sam held her breath and moved even closer. She bent down, ready to make her final leap and—

"What . . . ?"

Sam felt herself being pushed backward by someone who came *in between* her and the joker. As she tried to regain her footing, she saw a shimmering black cape, pale face, and pointed fangs.

Sam tried to circle around the caped figure, but a *second* vampire was right behind the first. And a third, and a fourth . . . There was a whole line of them!

No! she shouted in her mind. *You're ruining everything!*

Just as Sam pushed past the last vampire, the lights flickered and then came back on again. Finally, she could see the gravestone where she had first spotted the joker.

The joker was gone.

"Everything's okay, folks!" Travis called out. "Someone flipped the wrong switch."

Sam turned to face the line of vampires. Now that the lights were back on, she saw that the vampires' capes had been cut into gauzy, shimmering strips. They fluttered with every movement. Lips had been painted a deep red. Blood-red jewelry stood out against the white makeup covering the vampires' throats, arms, and ears. Some vampires had filmy bat wings that caught the beams of red, blue, and green lights. They went in a line, swooping and

REST IN PEACE

twirling in a circle around the central graveyard.

What is *this?* Sam wondered.

She walked quickly to the front of the line. When she saw the face of the lead vampire, she blinked in surprise.

"Amanda?" she asked. "What's going on?"

It was Amanda, all right. She smiled at Sam, showing blood-red lips and pointed fangs. "My dance, of course. Isn't it great?" Amanda said. She gave a dramatic sweep of her filmy, sparkling cape. "I *knew* you'd like it once you saw it for yourself."

She had to smile. She should have realized that Amanda wouldn't take no for an answer when she had been told she couldn't perform her special dance at the party. But Sam had to admit, the dance was great. A crowd of kids had already gathered to watch. They screamed with delight when Amanda's companion dancers looped around them, waving their gauzy capes.

"I thought you were going to do a *witches'* dance," Sam said.

"You're out of touch, Sam," Amanda told her. "You said yourself that witches wouldn't fit in with the Dracula theme. Besides, witches or vampires . . ." She gave a sweeping wave of her hand. "It hardly matters, as long as everyone gets to see *me* perform."

"Well, maybe you're right," Sam said, laughing. Obviously, *this* was the surprise Amanda had told her about. "That must be why you were prowling around the central graveyard yesterday," she said. "You were planning the dance."

Amanda nodded. "I had to find the best spot," she said. "The graveyard is perfect, don't you think?"

With that, Amanda started up her dance again. Shouts of excitement rang out. The party was back in full swing.

And the Halloween joker was still on the loose. . . .

"Are the lights going to stay off, or are they going to stay on?" Wishbone gazed up at the blue, green, and red spotlights that were aimed in different directions. "Can someone please make a decision here!"

Still, even if there *were* some technical difficulties, Wishbone thought the Halloween party was a big success. The young kids seemed to be having a great time. The volunteers were all pitching in to help make the party fun for them. And Wishbone was more than willing to do his fair share.

"Need any help with those refreshments, Joe?" Wishbone trotted over to the snack table. Joe stood behind it, handing out soft drinks, punch, juice, and cookies. "Maybe I'd better taste another one of those cookies . . . just in order to make sure that they're safe for humans to eat."

"You've had enough, Wishbone," Joe said. He smiled at a boy dressed as a superhero who stepped up to the table. "Here, have some ghoul-ade," Joe said, holding out a paper cup filled with a bright-red juice.

"Aha!" Wishbone pounced on some cookie crumbs that had fallen to the floor right next to the table. While he licked the last crumbly bits from his muzzle, he sat beneath the table and looked out at the party.

A purple dragon with yellow spots stood in front of Wishbone, waiting for Joe to hand out a soft drink. Looking past the floppy purple tail, Wishbone saw a two-headed monster. Beyond that was a vampire. . . .

"Nothing new there." Wishbone wagged his tail and gazed at the fanged creature. There were vampires all over Dracula's castle. In fact, almost all of the volunteers were wearing vampire costumes.

On second glance, though, Wishbone noticed this particular vampire was a *little* different. The costume had no cape. And, while most of the volunteers had simply painted their faces, this one had a mask with neon-green fangs that glowed from across the room.

"Nice canines," Wishbone said.

The vampire turned sneakily from side to side, then slipped behind a screen near the fire pole. Wishbone tipped his head to the side. "Hmm . . . there's something I don't trust about that vampire. . . ."

"Joe! You're not going to believe what just happened!" Sam said. She came hurrying up to the snack table. A worried frown was on her face. "It's the Halloween joker! He's here!"

"What!" Wishbone stiffened. All his senses went on red alert. "Where? Let me at him!" Then Joe circled from behind the table, and Wishbone ducked behind his legs. "Okay, you go first."

"You mean Curtis?" Joe asked. "How did *he* get into the party?"

"It's not Curtis. The real joker called and said we made a mistake when we caught Curtis," Sam explained. "The joker is here, and he's after *me.* I don't know who it is. All I saw were these green fangs . . ."

Wishbone didn't hear the rest of what Sam said. "I *knew* there was something about that vampire." He trotted in the direction of the fire pole, then paused to bark at Sam and Joe. "This way, you two. I'm on the joker's trail!"

Sam and Joe continued to talk seriously. They didn't even look in Wishbone's direction.

"Never mind. Tracking is a dog's job, after all. I'll fill you in when I get back."

Wishbone ran across the central graveyard, zigzagging around gravestones and wolves. As he neared the screen the joker had gone behind, Wishbone slowed down. Nose to the ground, he circled around the screen.

"Hmm . . . No joker here."

Wishbone did see some kids in costume next

to the fire pole. As the little dog watched the action, a dark figure suddenly swooped down the pole. Bats fluttered around him. The kids all screamed and jumped back. But Wishbone's keen eyes and nose told him this vampire wasn't the one he was after.

"Hi, Hank." Wishbone wagged his tail and gazed up at the caped figure who had just swooped down the pole. "Have you seen a sneaky-looking vampire with green fangs?"

Getting no answer from Hank, Wishbone backed away, his alert eyes sweeping over the area. "Hey . . . what's this?"

Wishbone felt his hind paws push against something hard. Turning around, he saw a telephone lying there.

"Hmm . . . Either this is a high-tech doggie chew toy, or a phone for humans that was dropped by mistake." Wishbone sniffed at the phone. Then he picked it up gently in his mouth. *Maybe whoever dropped it is the Halloween joker.*

Wishbone ran for the snack table.

"Sam!"

Chapter Twenty

Joe tugged at the collar of his vampire cape and peered out at the party. "I can't believe the joker is still here," he said to Sam.

"It's lucky that these little kids thought the blackout was part of the party," Sam said. "We've got to find the joker before someone *really* gets scared or hurt."

"You're right," Joe agreed.

He looked down as Wishbone appeared in front of the snack table.

"What do you have there, boy?" Joe asked.

Wishbone let something fall to the floor. Joe bent down to look at it.

"A phone," Joe said. He picked it up and held it out to Sam.

"A *cell* phone!" Sam's eyes lit up as she took it

from Joe. "The joker called me from *inside* the party just now. This must be what the joker used!"

"The joker must have dropped it," Joe pointed out. "But . . ."—he glanced at it, puzzled— ". . . what are *we* going to do with it?"

Sam glanced nervously over her shoulder. Joe had the feeling Sam expected the joker to strike at any moment, from any corner of Dracula's castle.

"What about the phone number we found yesterday?" he asked, as he handed out juice and cookies to two girls who were dressed as bats. "I bet the joker hid the cape and the piece of paper in the locker because he was planning to use it *tonight*. I mean, think about it. We found the cape in the locker. Now a vampire *without* a cape is going after you. I bet the cape was supposed to be part of the joker's costume. But now he has to do without it."

"You think the joker stored the cape *and* the number to use tonight?" Sam asked.

"Yes," Joe said. "I think we should dial the number again."

Sam flipped open the phone, turned it on, then punched in the telephone number.

"Let me talk to him," Joe said, holding out his hand. "It might catch him off guard." Sam gave Joe the phone as it was ringing, and he held it up to his ear. He heard a frantic boy's voice come over the line.

"It's about time you called!" the voice said. "This wolf suit is itching like crazy!"

Whoa! thought Joe. Whoever was on the line had obviously been expecting a call. Joe's guess was that the boy had been waiting to hear from the joker. Joe didn't want to tip the boy off to the fact that it was him and Sam calling. So he said nothing.

"Well," the boy went on, "are you ready for me to start?"

Joe didn't have to think very long about his answer. "Sure," he mumbled. Sam had said the joker's voice was low and muffled, so Joe tried to make his speech sound the same way.

To his relief, the boy on the line didn't question him. "I'm on my way," he said. Then Joe heard him hang up.

"We're in luck!" Joe turned the phone off and gave it back to Sam. He quickly told her what the boy had said. As she listened, her face grew more and more excited.

"So . . . the Halloween joker has a partner," she said. "Someone who is about to pull something, probably to throw us off guard." She frowned, glancing back at the central graveyard behind them. "That should give the joker the perfect chance to make his move against me."

"Right . . ." Joe now knew there were *two* people to worry about.

They had to remain calm and alert if they were to catch the pair.

"We have an advantage this time," Joe pointed out. "They have lost the advantage of surprise. Maybe we can come up with a plan of our own." Looking at Wishbone, he said, "Thanks for bringing us the phone, boy. It looks like you gave us a head start in finally trapping the joker."

Wishbone wagged his tail and looked up at Joe. "Happy to be of service."

"The first thing we should do is tell Mr. Del Rio what's going on," Sam said. "The younger kids might get really scared."

Joe wasn't sure where Travis was. He scanned over the different areas of Dracula's castle. But the screens made it impossible to see everywhere.

There were so many people, and so many costumes. Amanda and the other dancers were winding from one part of the castle to the next. And the colored lights and painted props made seeing very difficult.

"There's Mr. Del Rio," Sam said, pointing. "Over near Dracula's tomb."

The tomb was on the opposite side of the castle from the snack table. Joe strained to look and finally spotted Travis. He was standing outside the screen that separated Dracula's tomb from the rest of the castle. Joe made sure there were plenty of cookies and glasses of soft drinks, juice, and punch laid out for anyone who wanted them. Then he and Sam made their way across the store. They waited until Travis had finished guiding some kids into Dracula's tomb. Then they told him about all that had happened since the start of the party.

"So, *that's* why the lights went off," Travis said, shaking his head. "The switch box is behind the cash register. That's where all of the electrical equipment that controls the interior lights is. I thought it was just a case of one of the kids pulling the wrong switch." He frowned, crossing his arms over his chest. "So, Curtis is not the real joker. And if the real joker is here . . ."

"We've got to do something," Joe finished.

"We need to be ready to get the kids out of the way when the joker makes his move. They could be in danger." Sam said.

Travis nodded and said, "We've still got the Transylvania miniature-golf course set up out front. As soon as anything happens, I'll get all the kids out there to play. I'll need some help, though."

"I'll tell Hank and the other volunteers to be ready," Joe said. Turning to Sam, he added, "Why don't you find David and tell him what's been going on?"

"Good idea. Everyone else should make sure the kids are safe. Then you and David and I can make it our mission to deal with the joker," Sam said. Her eyes were filled with determination as she spoke. "In *Dracula,* Professor Van Helsing and Jonathan split up too."

"Divide and conquer," Joe said.

Sam nodded. "They knew Dracula was desperate—and very dangerous. They also knew that if they missed their chance to destroy him before he reached his castle, they would never get another one."

Sam tapped her chin thoughtfully, gazing at the line of vampires that wound past them.

"You know . . ." she said. "Maybe we should

warn Amanda, too. The dancers might be able to help."

"Sounds like a good plan," Travis said with a smile. "Let's do it."

Joe felt a new sense of hope and anticipation as he, Sam, and Travis scattered in different directions. It felt good to be *doing* something, instead of just waiting for the joker to strike.

"Come on, boy." Joe smiled down at Wishbone, who trotted along next to him. "Maybe we stand a chance against the joker after all."

"Okay, joker . . . I know you're out there." Wishbone trotted along next to the walls of Oakdale Sports & Games. His alert eyes scanned every area of Dracula's castle. "Why don't you and your fancy green teeth come out where we can see you?"

Wishbone didn't really expect the Halloween joker to show himself openly. The joker was too sneaky for that. But as long as Joe was busy getting the volunteers into position, Wishbone planned to stay on the lookout.

If I were a slippery trickster, where would I *hide?* Wishbone asked himself.

He tried to put himself in the joker's shoes. "Think sneaky . . . think *cat!*" But he simply couldn't do it. *"Yechh!"* Wishbone gave a shudder. "I guess I'll have to do this the canine way. . . ."

Wishbone felt a cool blast of air as he trotted past the entrance to the castle. All of a sudden, something huge and furry leaped through the castle's doorway. Wishbone spotted long ears, shaggy gray fur, a pointed snout, and sharp teeth.

"Hi, there!" Wishbone ran over to the wolf, barking. "My, what sharp teeth you have. . . ."

"Arrrraghh!" The wolf let out a piercing cry.

Kids jumped back, screaming and holding onto one another. But Wishbone just sat back and looked at the wolf.

"You're going to have to work on that howl, pal. Care to see how an expert does it?" Wishbone tilted back his head. But before he made any sound, the wolf leaped past him. "Hey! Not over there!" Wishbone barked. "You'll scare the kids!"

That seemed to be *exactly* what the wolf meant to do. He raced into the central graveyard, where a group of children were wandering among the gravestones and cardboard wolves. They all scattered, shrieking. The wolf in the costume let out another loud cry. But before he could move, Wishbone leaped toward him.

"Gotcha!" He clamped down on the wolf's tail with his teeth and pulled.

"Huh?" a muffled voice came from inside the wolf's mask. "Hey! Let go! Who *is* that?"

"Your worst nightmare—a dog with your tail in his mouth!" Wishbone gave another tug. Then he scrambled to keep the tail in his mouth as the wolf whirled around.

"This way, kids!" Wishbone heard Travis call out. "Last one out to the Transylvania golf course is a rotten pumpkin. And don't forget . . . there are prizes for everyone!"

Wishbone couldn't see Travis. He was too busy trying to keep his teeth firmly around the wolf's tail.

"Sam? Joe? David?" Wishbone couldn't bark, or he would lose his hold on the tail. But he hoped his friends were jumping into action.

You'd better be ready to make your move, Joe, the

terrier thought. *Because I'll bet the joker is about to make his—*

Joe had been talking to David inside Dracula's tomb when they had heard the loud cry. They had raced from the tomb just in time to see someone in a shaggy wolf's costume leap into the central graveyard.

"Way to go, Wishbone!" Joe said. Wishbone had the wolf by the tail. Joe could see Travis, Hank, and some other volunteers guiding the younger kids outside.

"Do you see Sam?" Joe asked, turning his head quickly from side to side. "We've got to keep an eye on her *and* find out who that wolf is."

"There she is!" David pointed toward the fire pole.

A quick glance told Joe that Sam was all right—for the moment. She was standing at the base of the fire pole, talking to Amanda. Joe noticed that she kept glancing over her shoulder.

"You keep an eye on her," he told David. "I'll be back as soon as I find out who that wolf is."

Joe ran toward the central graveyard. He saw that the wolf was making threatening gestures with his front paws. But with Wishbone hanging onto his tail, the wolf couldn't go anywhere.

"Hey wolf! How about picking on someone your own size?" Joe said as he came closer. "Like me."

"And me," a voice spoke up next to him.

Joe turned to see Amanda in her vampire costume. The other vampire dancers were with her. They swooped and howled, waving filmy capes and flashing red jewelry. They appeared to be twirling without any reason. But Joe noticed that they were circling around the wolf. Joe joined them as they moved closer, backing the wolf into the corner inside the entrance.

Joe whistled to Wishbone. "Good work, boy. But you can let go now," he said. "We've got him cornered."

The person's face was hidden behind the furry wolf's mask. But even after Wishbone let go of the tail, the wolf's steps were filled with panic. He kept jerking his head from side to side.

Suddenly, with a loud cry, the wolf twisted to the left and then pushed past Amanda.

"No!" Joe cried.

The wolf took off around the edge of the store. As he passed the table of refreshments, he pulled on the tablecloth. Refreshments spilled everywhere. Joe had to slow down to make sure he didn't slip. The wolf raced ahead.

"I'm after him, Joe!" David's voice rang out.

As Joe circled around the fallen cookies and beverages, he saw David racing across the central graveyard. The dancers were with him, but the wolf was a good few yards ahead. Joe saw a flash of gray as the creature raced past a creepy-looking cave to a door at the very back of the store. A furry paw reached for the doorknob. The door flew open, and the wolf disappeared on the other side.

Joe caught up to the others at the doorway. Inside, it was pitch-black. Joe ran his hands along the wall for a light switch, but he didn't find one. He heard footsteps coming from somewhere inside the dark space. Then there was a *thud,* and a voice cried out, "Ouch!"

"We're coming in after you," Joe said firmly. "And this time, we're going to get you."

Sam stood at the base of the fire pole. In a matter of seconds, Dracula's castle seemed to have emptied out.

It had all happened so quickly. One minute, she had been talking to Amanda about helping to capture the wolf. The next, the wolf was jumping into the castle. Sam felt as if someone had pressed a fast-forward button after that. Everything had happened in a blur—the dancers, the chase . . .

Now, Sam couldn't see a single person. As she looked out over the castle, she felt the hairs stand up on the back of her neck.

A soft shuffling noise made goose bumps pop out on her arms and legs.

"Joe? D-david?" she called out softly. But a feeling in her stomach told Sam that the noise wasn't coming from either of her friends.

Sam took a step forward. Then she gasped as something hit the floor right next to her. Suddenly, she was surrounded by a cloud of flashing sparks and smoke.

Sam closed her eyes for just a fraction of a second. But when she opened them again, the joker was there. He stood next to a large gravestone in the central graveyard, his green fangs glowing in the shadows.

"It's just me against you, Sam," he said, in the low, teasing voice she had come to know so well.

Then the vampire disappeared behind the gravestone. . . .

Chapter Twenty-One

Wishbone stood next to Joe in the dark room off the back of the store. He felt the warm heat of the people who had crowded into the space behind him and Joe. Ahead there was a stillness—broken only by the sounds the wolf made as he tried to make his way in the darkness. Wishbone still couldn't see. But he felt the hard concrete floor with his paws. He could smell oil, rubber, metal, and cardboard.

"Smells a lot like our garage at home, Joe!"

He heard Joe take a few steps, then brush his hands against something metallic. "Shelving," Joe muttered. "This must be some kind of storage space."

"Joe? Where are you!" David's voice spoke up from behind Wishbone.

"Right here," Joe said. "Let's spread out. That way, the wolf won't be able to get past us."

"Great idea, Joe!" Wishbone's keen eyes were starting to adjust to the darkness. He turned to gaze up at the black silhouettes of the volunteers. "Let's see a straight line, everyone. David, you first. Then Sarah, Amanda . . . You, too, Hank . . ."

Wishbone paused and cocked his head to one side. "Uh . . . everyone? Where's Sam?"

No one answered Wishbone's question. They were all too busy spreading out, he supposed. Wishbone trotted quickly from person to person, sniffing.

"That's not Sam. . . . *That's* not Sam. . . . Not Sam . . . Nope . . ."

When the terrier got to the last person, he still hadn't picked up Sam's special scent.

"Uh-oh . . . If we're all in here, and Sam *isn't* . . ." Wishbone gave an alarmed bark. "Joe, Sam is all alone in Dracula's castle with the Halloween joker!"

Sam took a deep breath. Her heart was pounding so loudly she thought surely the joker could hear it.

It's just me against you, Sam . . .

That voice . . . It was so creepy, so teasing and sure of itself.

Sam looked left, then right. Her eyes swept over the different areas of Dracula's castle—the central graveyard, the fire pole, the screen with the outside of Dracula's tomb painted on it. . . . She didn't see the joker. But she knew he could be hiding behind any of the screens, or in an area she couldn't see.

Sam shivered as her gaze came to the painted towers of Dracula's castle. There among the gravestones and the glowing yellow eyes of the wolves, she almost felt as if she had been carried off into the pages of *Dracula*.

She was beginning to understand exactly what Jonathan Harker must have gone through. He had been all alone, locked inside the castle with Count Dracula.

And here I am, alone with the joker. . . .

Sam rubbed her arms and tried to fight off the spooked feeling that had come over her. "You want to go one on one with me?" Sam said softly. "Well, here I come."

Taking a deep breath, she moved quickly to the central graveyard. An eerie green light shone over the headstones and wolves. A high-pitched howl echoed from the speakers. Sam moved quickly to the gravestone that the joker had disappeared behind.

"Gone," she murmured.

A sudden noise behind Sam made her jump. She whirled around and found herself facing a screen that had been painted to look like the forest near the front of Dracula's castle. Before she could take a step, the joker popped out from behind the screen. He let out a low laugh as he threw out his hands. All of a sudden something dark came flying through the air toward Sam.

Sam's cry of surprise was cut short as a sheet of netting fell over her head. The next thing she knew, her head and hands were tangled in the web. She kicked and flailed, but her movements only seemed to trap her even more.

"Trick . . . or treat . . ."

Sam gasped as the joker's voice spoke up right at her ear. Finally, the net was in a pile at her feet. Sam didn't know how she had managed to untangle herself. She spun toward the screen, but the joker was gone . . . again.

This time, Sam didn't hesitate. She ducked behind the screen where the joker had been. She drew in several gulping breaths of air, trying to calm herself down. She felt like a sitting duck,

1809

wandering around out in the open, waiting to be pounced on.

Think! she told herself. Somehow, Sam had to find a way to take the joker by surprise. That meant keeping out of sight, just as the joker was doing.

Sam moved quickly and quietly from one screen to the next. She kept low, and she changed directions several times. Except for a few shuffling noises, she didn't see or hear any sign of the joker. Hopefully, the joker didn't know where she was, either.

Okay, she thought, as she crouched behind David's game. *Now what?*

Keeping the joker from getting her wasn't going to be enough, Sam realized. She had to think of a way to *trap* the joker.

But how?

Sam tensed as she heard the soft sounds of footsteps coming from near the fire pole. She scooted slightly to the left so the joker wouldn't be able to see her. As she changed her position, she was startled by a flash of movement right next to her. Sam jumped—then let out her breath as she realized it was just her own reflection. The mirrors of David's game were placed in such a way that her own eyes stared back at her from endless different angles.

Then, as she gazed at the multiple reflections, an idea came to her. "That's it!" she whispered aloud.

Moving quickly and silently, Sam worked the mirrors free of David's game. There was one between each of the game's six targets. That meant five mirrors in all. *That ought to be plenty,* Sam thought.

She started toward Dracula's tomb with the mirrors tucked under her arm. She moved quietly, but not *too* quietly. This time, she *wanted* the joker to know where she was. With any luck, he would follow her.

Then, she would play a little joke of her own. . . .

Joe stared into the blackness in front of him. It was like a thick blanket. He couldn't see even a few feet in front of himself.

Reaching back, Joe shut the door that led to Dracula's castle. He wanted to make it as hard as possible for the wolf to escape.

Joe frowned as Wishbone let out a bark behind him. "Quiet, boy!" he said. It was the third time Wishbone had barked since they had followed the wolf to the back room. No doubt he felt anxious about the wolf's presence, too.

"Can everyone hold hands with the people on either side of them?" Joe said.

There were murmurs and rustling sounds. Joe was at one end of the line. With his right hand, he felt metal shelving that ran along the wall. When he reached to his left, his fingers touched Sarah's arm.

"Okay," he said. "Let's go."

Joe took one step forward, then another. He couldn't *see* the wolf. But sooner or later, he knew they were going to find him.

Joe heard the shuffling of the other party volunteers as they, too, moved forward. Knowing they were all working together gave him an added sense of strength. Sam had talked about the power of the good guys joining together in *Dracula*. Now he could feel it for himself.

Joe tensed as he heard something bang against a metal shelf ahead. "I hear you!" he called out. "You may as well give up now, before—"

There was a sudden flurry of noise. Footsteps, and then—

"Ooomph!" Joe felt the air knocked out of him as the wolf rammed into him in a head-on tackle.

He flew backward, letting go of Sarah as he fell under the weight of the wolf.

"Joe?" Sarah's worried voice called out.

"He's . . . here!" Joe managed to say.

Whoever was in the wolf costume was trying to scramble past Joe.

"Oh, no, you don't . . ." Joe muttered.

He grabbed the fake fur and held tight. Within seconds, Joe felt the other volunteers crowd around him and the wolf. There were shouts as hands reached out and grabbed the wolf's costume. Almost immediately, the wolf was caught.

"You're not going anywhere," Joe said. He grinned into the darkness. "Come on, everyone. Let's get this wolf out in the open where we can get a good look at him."

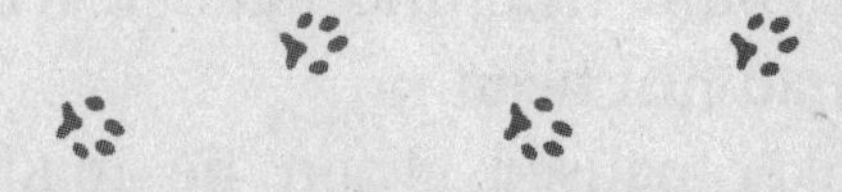

Sam crouched down behind Dracula's coffin.

Everything is in place, she thought. *Now, if the joker will just make his move . . .*

Sam looked at the small space between the coffin and the wall where the old firemen's lockers were. She had placed each of the five mirrors at different angles. They bounced reflections off one another. It created the same disorienting effect Sam had felt when she had played David's game.

She just hoped the joker would find the effect as confusing as she had. . . .

The seconds seemed to stretch out endlessly. Sam didn't know how long she had waited. Just when she was beginning to doubt whether the joker would come at all, she heard it—the soft sounds of the joker's footsteps. Sam heard him come into the tomb, then pause.

Here goes . . . she thought.

Sam poked her head around the side of the coffin and peeked out. "Boo!" she called. Then she ducked quickly back behind the coffin.

A quick shuffling told her the joker was following—right into her trap.

Sam slipped quietly around to one end of the coffin. She could hear the joker reach the spot where she had just been.

The joker paused. Then he made another move—and paused again.

"Huh?" he murmured.

Yes! Sam thought. Her plan was working perfectly!

She darted out from behind the coffin to find the vampire facing the mirrors. He turned one way, then another. Every time he moved, his green fangs jumped in endless different reflections.

Sam reached out and grabbed the vampire's arm. Before the joker could move, Sam reached for his mask with her other hand. She gave a yank and pulled the mask off. Suddenly, Sam was staring into a surprised—and very familiar—face.

It was Damont.

Chapter Twenty-Two

"Good work, guys! But there's still *one* little problem." Wishbone barked, scratching at the door that closed them inside the storage room. "Sam is still out there in the main room all alone!"

"We're coming, boy," Joe said, standing behind Wishbone in the darkness.

Wishbone heard the muttered complaints of whoever was wearing the wolf costume. Joe and the other volunteers were leading him toward the door. But Wishbone didn't stick around to see the furry mask come off. As soon as Joe opened the door, Wishbone raced to Sam's rescue.

"Don't worry, Sam! The canine patrol is on its way!"

The terrier ran, barking, past the bat-filled cave and into the central graveyard.

"Uh-oh . . ." Wishbone stopped short when he spotted some netting that was piled next to one of the screens. "I don't remember seeing that before. Sam . . . ?"

"I've got the joker, everyone!" Sam called out. "Over here!" Her voice came from the dark area underneath the stairs, where the old firemen's lockers were.

Wishbone raced past the screen that separated the area from the central graveyard. . . . "Yikes!" The terrier skidded to a stop and sat back on his haunches. "Sam? Why are there so many of you?" Wishbone cocked his head to one side, looking at the boy who stood next to Sam. "If I blink, will all those reflections go away? One of you is enough, Damonster!"

The next thing Wishbone knew, Joe and David appeared behind him.

"Sam, are you all right?" David asked.

Joe came over to Sam and looked at her with worried eyes. "Sam, are you okay? We got so caught up in catching the wolf, we forgot that you were—"

He broke off talking when his gaze landed on Damont. "*You're* the joker?" he asked.

Wishbone glanced up at the wolf Joe held by the arm. Wishbone saw that the furry mask was off. For the first time, he was able to see the person *inside* the costume. "Curtis, eh?"

"You two have a lot of explaining to do," Sam said. She looked back and forth between Curtis and Damont. "You went out of your way to shake up a lot of people."

Damont had been looking at the mirrors. But he turned suddenly and said, "Curtis just helped out with tonight's big prank. *I'm* the brains behind this attack."

Damont was very proud of being the joker—so proud that he didn't want to share the credit.

"So, tell me . . ." Wishbone gazed curiously up at Damont. "You think what you did is a *good* thing?"

"Why did you do it?" Joe asked.

Damont shrugged. "I figure I might as well leave my own special mark this Halloween."

"Sam was right," Joe said, shaking his head in disappointment. "You don't like having anyone else be the center of attention. So you decided to *steal* the limelight."

Wishbone barked at Damont. "Hey! I like a little attention myself. A simple flip usually does the trick."

"You should have seen your face when that skeleton dropped out of the tree, Talbot," Damont said with glee. "I guess I got you really spooked with the phone call I made before I did that."

"That's another thing," Sam said, frowning. "Why did you call *me* before every practical joke?"

"It was an accident the first time," Damont explained. "When I telephoned the store, you answered. After that, I figured, why not call you *every* time? It was kind of cool making it a battle of wits between us, seeing how many times I could outsmart you."

"You didn't exactly play fair, Damont," David pointed out. "You set me up to be a suspect when you took the dry ice and tape recording from my workshop. And why did you have to smash Sarah's pumpkin?"

Wishbone saw an embarrassed look come into Damont's eyes. "That was a mistake," the boy admitted. "All I wanted to do was make that fog, then scare her with the recording of the creepy laugh. I knocked the pumpkin over by accident when I ran to get away."

"Then you put the tape recorder back in David's garage, so people would think *he* was the joker," Joe finished. "You even set *yourself* up as a victim, so we wouldn't suspect you."

"I remember seeing you at Pepper Pete's, right after the joker called and hinted that you would be the victim," Sam said. She looked at Damont through narrowed eyes. "I *knew* there was something funny about the way you were acting that night. I should have trusted my feelings."

"How did you get the costume from Amanda?" Joe asked.

"I saw her throw it away at school, so I took it. I knew I'd find the right time to use it. And when you caught up with me outside Pepper Pete's, you gave me the perfect chance, Sam," Damont explained. He gave one of his superior smiles. "You didn't even question me when I suggested that we separate. Then, while I was behind Oakdale Sports and Games, I purposely stashed the witch's hat at the fence." He let out a laugh, shaking his head. "You never suspected a thing!"

"You knew Sam would try to protect you from the joker. Most people would appreciate someone looking out for them," Joe said angrily. "But you used it as a weapon against her."

Wishbone sat back and gazed at Damont. "Is there no end to your dirty deeds?"

"I was sure something wasn't right when you and Curtis showed up to help with the party," Sam said, shaking her head in anger. "You never really wanted to help at all. Did you? You just came to check everything out so you could set things up for tonight."

Damont's smile was starting to fade.

Wishbone followed the boy's gaze as it traveled from face to face. "What's the matter, Damont? People aren't as impressed with your clever tricks as you thought they would be?" Wishbone barked up at the boy.

"I never figured anyone would look in those old firemen's lockers," Damont said. "I hid the cape for my costume back there. . . ."

"And you did the same thing with the telephone number for the pay phone down the street,

where Curtis would be waiting for you to call him," Joe finished. He reached down to pat Wishbone. "Thanks to Wishbone, we got both of those pieces of evidence."

"I've got the nose for the job, after all." Wishbone gave a happy bark, smiling up at Joe and wagging his tail.

"Yeah, well . . ." Damont glanced around the tomb. He looked exactly the way Wishbone felt when Wanda caught him digging in her flower beds. Things obviously weren't working out the way the prankster had expected they would.

"You're the one who turned off all the lights tonight," David guessed. "Once you realized you didn't have the number to call Curtis, you had to create your own way of throwing us off the track."

Damont gave a nod, frowning. "Mr. Del Rio got the lights back on faster than I expected. I guess I must have dropped my cell phone then, too."

"You mean, this?" Sam pulled the cell phone from the back pocket of her jeans.

When Damont caught sight of it, his mouth dropped. "How did you . . . ?"

"Wishbone found it," Sam told him. "This gave us exactly the clue we needed to figure out what your plan was," she said.

"Hey! I need that!" Damont said.

She held the phone for a moment. Then she gave it to Damont.

"It belongs to my parents," Damont said. "They'll be really angry with me if they find out I borrowed it without asking." He let out a sigh of relief, tucking it into his pants pocket. "At least I didn't lose it."

"You've got the phone . . ." Wishbone barked out to Damont. "But your troubles are far from over, Mr. Joker. Something tells me you're going to be on a tighter leash from now on. . . ."

When Joe got out of bed on Saturday morning, the first thing he did was look out his bedroom window. It was another perfect fall morning—sunny and cool, with clear blue skies. There had been a series of day just like it. But Joe hoped that today would be different in at least one way.

"I'm glad the Halloween joker has been caught," he said aloud. Joe reached down to pat Wishbone, who was still curled up at the end of his pal's bed. "Now things can get back to normal. No more feeling as if something bad is going to happen. No more overactive imagination painting creepy pictures of the Murphy house."

Wishbone stretched out his front legs, wagging his tail. Then he jumped to the floor, ran to the bedroom door, and barked.

"I'm hungry, too, Wishbone," Joe said, laughing. "Come on. Let's go downstairs."

He found a note from his mother on the dining room table:

> Went grocery shopping.
> Back soon.
>
> Love,
> Mom

Joe had just poured kibble into Wishbone's dish when the doorbell rang. When Joe went to the door and opened it, he was surprised to see Sam and David standing there.

"Hi, Joe," Sam said, smiling. "I hope you didn't eat breakfast yet. We brought you some fresh muffins and hot chocolate."

"Great!" Joe said.

David stepped into the hallway behind Sam. He held up a large paper bag. "We figured we deserved to celebrate, now that the Halloween joker has been caught," he said.

After they went into the kitchen, they began to set everything out on the table. Joe thought about all that had happened the last few days. He felt proud of the way he and Sam and David had taken action. They had gone after the joker, and his accomplice, and stopped them.

"It figures that the joker was Damont," he said, biting into a blueberry muffin.

"At least we caught him and Curtis," David said. "And they're paying for the trouble they caused."

Travis Del Rio had come up with the idea for the boys' punishment. The two boys had been given the job of taking Dracula's castle apart and doing a thorough cleanup of the store. They were also going to clean up after the scavenger hunt next week on Halloween night, as well.

"While they're busy cleaning today, *we* can start getting into high gear for Halloween," Sam said, grinning. "Maybe we could start planning our costumes for the scavenger hunt."

As soon as Sam started to talk about Halloween, Joe felt his mouth dry up. There it was again—the same thought that something bad might happen.

So much for taking control, he thought. *How could I feel this way even* after *we've caught Damont and Curtis?*

"How about it?" David asked, turning toward

Joe. "Do you want to go to the scavenger hunt with Sam and me?"

"I'll see . . ." Joe said with hesitation.

He didn't want to let down Sam and David. But he felt as if there had already been enough trouble the last few days. He wasn't in the mood for any more.

Maybe, he thought, *I'll just skip celebrating Halloween this year.*

Sam took a sip of hot chocolate, then reached for a second muffin. "We don't have to decide about the scavenger hunt yet," she said. "Right now, I'm happy just knowing that I didn't make a mistake—I was right to believe that the people around me are basically good."

"Even Damont?" David asked.

Sam nodded. "Even him," she said. "I know he scared a lot of people. And he definitely went too far with his pranks. But Damont isn't a bad person. I think that in a weird way, he meant his practical jokes to be fun—to get us all into the spirit of Halloween."

David rolled his eyes and said, "Fun for *him,* maybe."

"I guess I know what you mean," Joe said to Sam. "Damont was just being Damont. But that's not nearly as bad as being, say, Dracula."

"Exactly," Sam said. "And, trust me, Damont is getting off a lot easier than Dracula did."

David looked across the table at Sam. "Oh, really?" he asked. "How does the book end?"

Sam took a deep breath. She had just finished the book the night before, when she had returned home after the party. The end had been so thrilling that she was still thinking about it.

"Well," she began, "I don't want to give the ending away, but let's just say that Dracula made a dramatic exit. But he had lived a long time, and his evil went back a long way. Dracula was really a symbol for the evil that still exists in the world."

"Wylie Savage is proof that it does," Joe said, frowning.

At that, Wishbone lifted his head from his food dish and gave a bark. If Sam didn't know better, she would have thought he was agreeing with them.

"But what's important," Sam went on, grinning from ear to ear, "is that the good guys *do* win in the end."

About Anne Capeci

Anne Capeci has written more than a dozen mysteries for children and young adults. Many of her mysteries feature young detectives, but none with as much fur as Wishbone. Anne has written two books for the WISHBONE Mysteries series, *The Maltese Dog* and *Key to the Golden Dog*. She was pleased to have the opportunity to write the first WISHBONE Super Mysteries title, *The Halloween Joker*.

Anne thought that *Dracula*, Bram Stoker's classic vampire novel, would be the perfect story to explore in *The Halloween Joker*. She has never encountered a more chilling, evil character than Count Dracula. In the novel, Dracula invades the lives of innocent people—young men and women whose lives are filled with happiness and hope. Once Dracula slips in among them, infecting them with his evil blood, their basic belief in the goodness of mankind is shaken.

Anne was impressed with the way those good men and women refused to back down in the face of Dracula's tremendous dark powers. Writing *The Halloween Joker* gave her a chance to consider how

Sam, Joe, David, and Wishbone would react when evil invaded their world.

Anne lives in Brooklyn, New York, with her husband and their two children. She has seen several vampires at her local annual Halloween parade, including her own son! Fortunately, their most evil deed was eating too much candy.